THE SHIP
OF SECRETS

THE SHIP OF SECRETS

JOHN LILITH

Copyright © 2021 John Lilith

The moral right of the author has been asserted.

Apart from any fair dealing for the purposes of research or private study, or criticism or review, as permitted under the Copyright, Designs and Patents Act 1988, this publication may only be reproduced, stored or transmitted, in any form or by any means, with the prior permission in writing of the publishers, or in the case of reprographic reproduction in accordance with the terms of licences issued by the Copyright Licensing Agency. Enquiries concerning reproduction outside those terms should be sent to the publishers.

This is a work of fiction. Names, characters, businesses, places, events and incidents are either the products of the author's imagination or used in a fictitious manner. Any resemblance to actual persons, living or dead, or actual events is purely coincidental.

Matador
9 Priory Business Park,
Wistow Road, Kibworth Beauchamp,
Leicestershire. LE8 0RX
Tel: 0116 279 2299
Email: books@troubador.co.uk
Web: www.troubador.co.uk/matador
Twitter: @matadorbooks

ISBN 978 1800464 773

British Library Cataloguing in Publication Data.
A catalogue record for this book is available from the British Library.

Printed and bound in Great Britain by 4edge Limited
Typeset in 11pt Minion Pro by Troubador Publishing Ltd, Leicester, UK

Matador is an imprint of Troubador Publishing Ltd

For Xiujing

ACKNOWLEDGEMENTS

I wish to express my gratitude to the peoples of all countries of the globe for the richness of their folk songs, many of which emanate from an oral tradition and therefore have numerous variants. The few I have included in this narrative are represented in a manner that is faithful to the cultures whence they came.

Thank you also to the mariners of the world for their own tradition of singing work songs, popularly known as sea shanties.

And finally, a special thanks to Joseph Conrad, sailor and novelist, whose inspiring works of greatness set me to spinning this nautical yarn.

John Lilith

ONE

THE DARKNESS

It is after midnight, and the moon is high over the dark and silent port. A gentle land breeze pervades the air, and yellow lights can be seen in the windows of the tavern. The chatter of revellers has long since faded, as almost everyone has gone home now. Suddenly, the tavern's door is flung open. Cuttleson, looking sharp-featured and intense, emerges onto the quiet street. He feels heavy with the evening's drinking.

This is not his usual condition.

He sallies forth into the night. Lurching around the corner and onto the quay, he pauses a moment to take in the silence. In his inebriated state, he calls out to the darkness: 'Make way there.' Gathering speed, he steers himself as steadily as his tired legs will permit.

Follow discreetly with me. Let us see where he goes.

Cuttleson continues to make his staggering headway, cursing as he goes. 'Damn them, those pirate skull-a-bones.' He spits, and spits again. After a short distance, he cuts his speed and comes to a stop alongside the gangplank of The Buccaneer. She is a brig that has taken a mooring a week ago and has not put to sea again since. 'Come out, you blitherings!' he bawls. 'Come out, I say, or I'll split your gizzards with this scrimshaw knife!' He pauses, teetering on the edge of the quay. 'You won't show yourselves? Well then, I'll come aboard, and I'll have your guts for garters!'

The Buccaneer, however, has been left unguarded. For the last three days no watch has been posted, and the tavern regulars have not seen any of the pirate crew passing by on the way to the Blue Parrot for a few tankards. Perhaps they have killed one another fighting over tobacco, or the division of spoils. Who knows where the sea-dogs have gone?

Cuttleson charges across the gangplank as fast as his legs can carry him, then pauses a moment as his feet hit the deck. He decides to make his way for'ard and sticks his head into the gloom of the fo'c'sle. He hears nothing. Then he slowly begins to scour the maindeck. He searches here, there and everywhere, but cannot find a living soul. With a growing conviction that the ship may be deserted, he stows the knife safely in his jacket and makes his way aft to the crew's accommodation. On entering the sleeping quarters, he feels his way around in the darkness. Here too, no-one is present.

What he fails to see and cannot hear during his search, is the strange figure passing noiselessly behind him. It is a hideous, deathly wraith, shimmering in the gloom as it drifts silently up the companionway, then disappears.

Cuttleson has, however, sensed the cold and clammy presence aboard the ship. Feeling the hairs on the back of his neck standing on end, he spins round so fast he falls over backwards into a bunk.

Within moments he is a snoring, sleeping lump. In his dream state, his seeing mind begins to wander amidst an undiscovered sea of shapes, of suckered tentacles that reach out to him, of sea anemones waving, as if to warn him: 'Take care, take care.' Antennaed creatures walk mysteriously on the sandy sea bed, seeking comfort amongst corals. He is carried along, spinning and swirling weightlessly with arms and legs akimbo, in that silent strangeness of the deep, until he finally comes to rest by Davy Jones's Locker.

We will part company from our adventurer for now. He will be out of his slumbers by the time the sun is over the yardarm. Let us slip away, and leave him to his dreams...

TWO

INCIDENT IN THE TAVERN

The taverners were sitting around, enjoying the drinks and entertainment. Melodious sounds hung in the air. The Musician, standing at his usual spot in the cosy, was singing a particularly wistful version of "Rosin-the-Bow" and accompanying it with his violin-playing.

One member of the appreciative audience, however, had a thought on her mind that was bothering her. She said quietly to a friend, 'Where's Cuttleson? I haven't seen him all week.'

'Don't be worryin' about him,' her friend replied. 'It'll have somethin' to do with that ship he mentioned. He'll be all right. He always is.'

This sparked a murmured discussion among several regulars seated close to them.

'Not every pirate has disappeared, you know,' said one.

'How so?' said his companion.

'I did see one of them yesterday. The one they call Snargel – with the eye patch and a hooped earring through the left ear.'

'Oh, him!' said a fellow imbiber. 'Nasty! Permanent sneer on his face. And 'ave you seen them clothes? Ridiculous! Cropped pirate pants, and that striped top with um…a sort of…reefer jacket that looks to be about two sizes too big. Ha! Stole it, I reckon. I'd put my money on it!'

'Probably murdered for it,' said another. 'And the buckled shoes. You can hear 'em going ching-ching, ching-ching, everywhere he walks.'

'And what about that cutlass?' said the first. 'We had better keep our distance from him.'

'Where did you see him anyway?' the friend asked.

'He was going in the door of the Blue Parrot – wanting more rum, I expect. Wonder if I should go and find Cuttleson, and tell him?'

'Oh, no!' pleaded Fanny. 'You know what could happen!'

'Yes, I do. He might kill Snargel.'

'And then Cuttleson may be hanged!' gasped Fanny.

'Perhaps he don't care about that, an' all,' piped up another. 'He just seems to want every last one o' that Buccaneer crew dead, no matter what.'

This last toper, who had thrown several ales down his throat already this evening, paused to put down his drink, and took a deep breath before giving his final verdict. He stood up. 'Dead!' he announced dramatically to a startled audience. 'Dead as the proverbial Dodo. Extinction, I tell you.'

At that moment the street door was flung open, and the dreaded Snargel himself appeared. He stood just inside the doorway, his beady one-eyed gaze slowly surveying the assembly.

Each of the regulars in turn felt the cold stare fixing on him, or her, just for a moment, before it passed on to the next person. Next, the fiddle music faltered, and then died away completely, as Snargel's cruel gaze took in the Musician for a second or two. Then the roving eye moved on, encompassing the whole company in its glare again.

No-one dared to move a muscle.

'Wheere – is – he?' the pirate snarled, gripping the handle of his cutlass.

Alas, Snargel had misjudged the situation. Without warning, Cuttleson suddenly appeared behind him in the doorway, and in one bound was upon him, knocking Snargel over and pinning him to the floor, face down.

Cuttleson drew his knife, and with his knees in the severely winded pirate's back, grabbed hold of him by the hair and pressed the blade against the back of Snargel's right ear. 'This,' he shouted, 'is for Fanny's mother, and the doubloons!' In one swift stroke he sliced off Snargel's ear. Thus detached, it fell onto the stone floor.

But Cuttleson was not finished with his adversary yet. He held the point of the knife under the pirate's one good eye and said, slowly and deliberately, 'If I ever see you in this town again, I'll do for your remaining ocular cavity as well. Mark that, Snargel, and don't forget it!' With that, he dragged the bleeding pirate to his feet and disarmed him, throwing the cutlass out of reach.

Fanny, in tears now at having witnessed such violence, ran to the bar and fetched towels, which she gave to the pirate to help staunch the blood streaming down his neck. Cuttleson, without another word, spun Snargel around and frogmarched him out of the doorway, and quickly away, in the direction of the quay.

Night-time fell once more upon their world, and the regulars went off to their homes. Except, that is, for The Musician, who took up his violin once more. Standing in the middle of the empty cosy, he gave a rendering of "The Rover", tapping a foot in rhythm as he played.

The next day, it was heard around the waterfront that Snargel, one-eyed and one-eared, had appeared briefly on the quayside early that morning with his head bandaged. He had boarded a sloop that had put into Port Guardian at first light to take on provisions of hardtack, vegetables, fruit, fresh water, and rum. She was bound for the Spanish Main. He had joined the crew. The ching-ching, ching-ching of his buckled shoes along the wharf and across the sloop's gangplank, had been heard for the last time in Port Guardian.

※

It was some days later.

The sweet evening breeze whispered its way down the hillsides and into the port, where the locals could be found gathered in the cosy as usual. The Musician, standing at his spot, put down the violin alongside his guitar, stood in silence a moment, and then began a folk song unaccompanied. His vibrant tones filled the room with that song of Scotland, "The Wild Mountain Thyme".

The assembled regulars sat about, enjoying their favourite tipples: a Tia Maria here, an Irish whiskey there, and more than a few ales. Amidst the company sat Cuttleson. One taverner, seated close by, looked up from contemplation of his drink and said to him, 'Why such enmity between you and those pirate fellows?'

'They are low life,' replied Cuttleson flatly, 'and an anachronism, to boot. We need to be rid of them. They are sea-robbers and nothing more.' He wiped his mouth with his hand. 'They continue to live out their own rotten history on the high seas, even as I speak. I loathe them for their greed, brutishness and thieving.'

Members of the company looked at one another. Then one shook his head and said, 'But you aren't telling us the whole story, Cuttleson. I was there the other night.'

'What night?'

'The night you did for Snargel. I heard you shout: "This is for Fanny's mother!" What did you mean?'

'I don't want to talk about that.' Cuttleson glanced around again. 'Where *is* Fan tonight, anyway?'

Another of the company spoke up. 'One or two of the women 'ave been buyin' new dresses, and she went with 'em today. She'll be back at one o' their houses by now, I reckon; tryin' on somethin' new for herself.'

Cuttleson lapsed into silence. He'd begun thinking about Fanny's mother again.

INCIDENT IN THE TAVERN

The Musician reached the final refrain with the words "Will Ye Go, Lassie, Go?" A ripple of approval came from the audience, and they gave a round of applause.

What happened next was rather strange. They heard a tapping from outside, and every window along the quayside wall of the tavern seemed to shake. The atmosphere inside suddenly became colder as a chill spread through the room. Then it dissipated just as quickly.

'Hey, what was that?' said one of the regulars.

'I'll go and check it out,' said Cuttleson. He got up and made for the door.

Once outside, he looked this way and that, took a few paces to the end of the street, then turned the corner and went off along the quay, passing several of the ships moored there.

In the twilight, he came to the two-masted sailer that he knew of old. The brig was surging a little at her moorings, as a swell had got up. As he approached, he was just able to perceive in the dusk the shape of a tall shimmering figure which at that very moment was making its way across the gangplank. It seemed as it did so to hover above the planking as it boarded the vessel. Cuttleson sensed something ethereal. Yet, at the same time, he noticed something familiar about its bearing. He thought for a moment, then broke into a smile as a realization came to him in the gathering darkness. 'That's the way back,' he murmured to himself. He turned and walked back along the quay, while considering the prospect further, and re-entered the tavern.

One of the frequenters put down his drinking pot and called out to him, 'What was goin' on out there?'

'Oh, it's nothing to worry about,' replied Cuttleson. 'Just a nor'easter starting to blow. Look, I'll have to be going.'

Having put the company at their ease, he left.

The Musician took up his guitar this time, and began another song, his final one of the night. As the regulars started putting on their coats and began their unsteady exit from the tavern, he sent them on their way with his wistful rendering of "The Water Is Wide".

'Oh, the water is wide, I cannot cross over,
Neither have I wings to fly,
Give me a boat, that will carry two,
And both shall row, my love and I…'

The next morning would see preparations being made for The Buccaneer to put to sea.

THREE
A SHIP AT SEA

The ship had been at sea for some weeks. She had crossed the Bay of Biscay, rounded Cape Finisterre, then continued down the Atlantic seaboard. Keeping sight of the High Atlas on the port beam, she had sailed south past The Azores, and then The Canaries, and had crossed the latitude of the Tropic of Cancer. Making the most of a fair wind off the coast of Senegal, she was drawing nearer each day to the islands off Cape Verde.

This voyage, ever sou'sou'west, was being directed by the pointing finger of The Wraith. The ship rolled in the swell and continued to make good headway. The sea wind freshened the air and the faces of the crew.

Cuttleson, having added the role of quartermaster to his other maritime preoccupations, was seated in what had been the captain's cabin. He was considering what had been achieved so far. Four personnel had signed on in

Port Guardian. He had been lucky to find even these, as he needed men with certain special characteristics and skills for the task ahead.

First, there were the two Russians. Brodnov, a giant of a man, as weathered as the timbers of The Buccaneer herself. Then came Nevsky, a true mariner, experienced in every aspect of the seafaring life. Next, there was the Chinese cook, Chang. He had seen many years of service on junks in the East China Sea, both as a ship's cook and as a seaman, before venturing to other continents. And then there was the youth, Tom. Cuttleson had been reluctant at first to take a chance on such an inexperienced youngster, but the lad had approached him and clearly wanted to prove himself. A runaway with a thirst for adventure, he had expressed a willingness to learn, and so he got taken on.

This unique assortment, plus Cuttleson himself, was made up to a ship's complement of just six souls by The Wraith. This last was once a certain Captain Joseph Clinker, whose spirit abroad came cloaked and hooded. He – or it – spent its days up for'ard on the fo'c'sle, staring ahead at the great ocean before it. From time to time it would also take to drifting back and forth along the maindeck, seeming on those occasions to be in thought awhile, before returning once more to its chosen station.

Cuttleson looked at the mid-Atlantic chart. Before they left Port Guardian, he and The Wraith had pored over charts together. The Wraith had first pointed with a bony finger at the Cape Verde Islands that lie off West Africa. It had then swept a ghostly hand across the ocean, westwards as far as the Caribbean. It had let its forefinger hover over that sea.

From this scant information, Cuttleson had calculated what would be needed for a voyage of several weeks, perhaps months. He had provisioned the ship accordingly. At the same time, he had added to the ship's existing stock of gunpowder and cannonballs a number of other important items, such as grapeshot, new wadding, fuses, patches, squibs and pistols. He had also taken the cutlasses that he'd found in deck lockers, to a cutler who honed them to a lethal degree of sharpness.

The Buccaneer in her seafaring lifetime had been modified several times. Firstly, by merchants of the rum and tobacco trade, and then by sugar and cotton traders, and finally by the pirates who had stormed her. Those scheming sea-dogs, having taken a considerable liking to their prize, had sailed her to an obscure, out-of-the-way shipyard; and in that place where no questions are asked, had installed ten gun-ports and cannon to suit their nefarious designs. Brazenly, they had also kept an ensign flying.

She was still a sturdy vessel of course, and Cuttleson had found on internal inspection that she had sprung no leaks. He was thankful, as this ship would now have to sail another thousand leagues.

Chang stuck his head through the cabin doorway. 'Haa, boss! You like chow mein? Have some chicken and noodle, eh?'

'Why, thank you, Mr. Chang,' replied the quartermaster. 'Mind if I give up on the chopsticks though? I still cannot get used to them. Just a fork will do if you please.'

'No chopsticks for Mr. C.,' said the cook, making a mental note of the order. He disappeared briefly, then returned to the cabin with the steaming dish. 'Here's plenty chow! And some lychees I put on small plate, right here.' He went back to the galley and continued arranging generous portions for the rest of the crew.

Nevsky was stationed at the helm. Brodnov was walking around the maindeck, checking the set of the sails, all fastenings, and anything else that might need attention. The deck caulking still looked quite sound. Tom was experimenting with the swivel gun at the rail, aiming its long, trumpet-like barrel at imaginary foes.

Chang came out from the galley calling out 'Chop time! Tom, you take this one to Mr. Nevs. Mr. Brods, here you are.'

'Da, Chang. Comin' right zap now!' said Brodnov, slapping his great hands together demonstrably. A curious idiosyncrasy of his, it was a habit he often displayed to show his readiness for anything in the offing.

The wind freshened again, the sails billowed their approval, and the vessel followed her course with renewed zeal. The Buccaneer would make harbour at Praia, Cape Verde Islands, on the morrow. She would take on fresh water, further supplies of fresh fruit and vegetables, chickens in cages, salt pork, coffee, tea, a sack of sugar, and casks of rum. Any necessary sail repairs would also be made good during the stay.

Evening came on, and a myriad of stars began to twinkle. Port and starboard lamps in their lanterns were lit, and a white masthead light was hoisted. The bell was sounded. Brodnov appeared, wrapped in a boat cloak. He came on watch and took the helm. The rest of the crew, few as they were, turned in.

All except The Wraith. Later, this spirit of the captain commenced its nightly wanderings fore and aft, in the same way that Joseph Clinker had often done in his earthly lifetime.

Brodnov, his hands firmly on the wheel, tried to pay the unearthly spirit no heed during the night watch. He was a seasoned mariner just like Nevsky, remaining steadfast in the face of any challenge. He did, however, experience a certain chill whenever the thing passed close by him.

The Wraith eventually returned to the fo'c'sle head, and took up its position once more, as the eternal watcher of the night sky.

FOUR

MISS FANNY CLINKER

In the tavern at Port Guardian, the evening's entertainment was in full swing, and quite a crowd was in attendance. The kitchen was busy, and the bar was besieged with orders. The company was very vocal.

The Musician, presenting himself on this occasion as one half of a duo with his associate, had earlier recounted a traditional tale of sibling rivalry, "Two Sisters". Next, they had entertained the audience with the story of "The Wild Colonial Boy".

Following several more accomplished performances, they brought the assembled company to their feet with the lively "Camptown Races". This seemed to be the moment for folk-dancing. The keenest came forward and began to form up. Fanny, in her long dress, sequined shoes and ribboned hair, joined them. The music played on merrily, and the participants danced on, ever more wildly. One or two began to get a little giddy.

The Musician judged this a suitable opportunity to announce a short break. The next fifteen minutes saw a general clamour at the bar by those most eager for refills, while dancers sat down to catch their breath.

The players returned refreshed, settled the audience down once more, and began a sweet rendering of an altogether gentler Irish ballad, about a street-hawker selling shellfish from a cart in the 1870s, or even the 1790s or earlier still, by some accounts. It was the song of "Mary Malone":

'In Dublin's fair city,
Where the girls are so pretty,
I first set my eyes on sweet mistress Malone.
She wheeled her wheelbarrow,
Through the streets broad and narrow,
Crying oysters, and cockles, and mussels for sale.'

The audience gave the refrain -

'Crying oysters, and cockles, and mussels for sale.'

During this plaintive, Fanny slipped out to take in the fresh evening air for a while and decided to walk a little way along the dark quayside. She paused and stood there a moment, looking into the infinite blackness of the sea.

The sadness that had briefly been shaken off, suddenly returned and overcame her. She whispered into the void: 'God bless you and keep you safe, Cuttleson.' Wiping the tears from her eyes, she turned away and walked slowly back to the tavern.

FIVE

CLIMBING THE RIGGING

In the western Atlantic, The Buccaneer sailed onward beneath a clear blue sky. Her course was now due west. She had come onto this bearing weeks ago, on leaving Cape Verde. During that short stay at Praia, a seventh crew member had joined ship.

This latest recruit, referred to as Ratter by the others, spent some of the daylight hours pacing the maindeck and gun-deck, but preferred to spend the nights down in the hold, while the rest of the crew – except for The Wraith and the watch duty – were sleeping.

Now, in the heat of the day, the quartermaster appeared on the poopdeck. He came and stood beside Brod, who had the helm. Cuttleson squinted at the noonday sun high in the sky. He took measurements with the sextant, and from his observations jotted down the latest figures. He re-checked the angle of elevation from the horizon.

Nev, who was on the fo'c'sle, gave a sidelong glance at The Wraith and continued to uncoil some of the rope in his hands, whilst letting the float hang freely. He waited for the quartermaster's signal.

Cuttleson raised his arm.

Nev cast the float over the starboard bow and into the sea, allowing the line to pay itself out freely.

Cuttleson, peering over the side, counted the seconds until it had travelled the length of the ship and passed below him at the stern. He then signalled again to Nev, who quickly began hauling it in. They repeated the procedure.

The Wraith remained motionless, as was its wont, two orbs gazing fixedly at the empty horizon. Nev gave it another passing glance, then came aft.

Brod called out to Tom, who was standing on the maindeck. 'Get aloft! Dat fore tops'l reef should be loosed, dammit!'

Tom hesitated as to which sail was meant, and the seaman shook a fist at him.

'Get up dat riggin' zap quick, or I throw ya t'da sharkses!'

Cuttleson intervened immediately. 'Stop it, or I will see to it that you become a meal for the sharks yourself, and they'll be feeding on you for a week!'

Brod, his bald slavic head shining in the sun, glowered at Tom and gripped the wheel so tightly his knuckles turned white. After Cuttleson's reprimand, however, he said nothing more.

But Cuttleson was not quite finished with him. 'Save your temper until we get there. It'll be needed later.' Then he called out to the youth. 'Do as the able seamen tell you, Tom. Get aloft on the foremast there, at the double.'

Tom clambered up the rigging. The rolling of the vessel became more exaggerated the higher he went. By the time he reached the tops'l yard, he found himself swaying out over the sea to port, only to veer right over to starboard moments later, and then sway back again. He struggled to loosen the ties at first, and then managed to do it. He began carefully to feel his way back down until his feet were in contact with the deck. It took a few moments for the dizziness that had suddenly come over him while aloft, to wear off.

Cuttleson addressed Tom once more. 'It's nearly chop time. Go to the galley now and help Mr. Chang.'

Tom steadied his gait on the rolling deck and made his way aft. The aroma of dumplings and noodles was emerging from the galley. Just before he entered, he looked back at the quartermaster.

Cuttleson, who had been watching Tom and saw the glance, gave a smile and called out once more, this time to reassure the youth. 'You did well, Mister!'

Tom was beaming as he entered the cook's domain.

The quartermaster returned to stand beside Brod at the helm again.

Brod asked, 'How long t'da Caribbee now, Mr. C.?'

'If we maintain this rate of knots and do not deviate from the 15° parallel,' replied Cuttleson, 'we are sure to sight the Windward Isles in three more days. Maintain due west.'

'Aye, sir.'

Sea spray came up and showered its saltiness over the vessel and her crew. A shoal of flying fishes appeared. They began their playful dance in and out of the swell, their silvery shapes glinting in the sun.

SIX

MARTINIQUE

The ship sailed on, ever westwards, under a tropical sky. The trade winds had been constant. She had been tested by nothing more than an occasional squall.

The crew were swarthy and weather-beaten, and all except bald Brod had long straggly hair. Cuttleson, rough-chinned from constant knife-shaving and coarse soap, had the helm. Nev was perched aloft in the crow's nest, his eyes fixed on the horizon. The Wraith was on the fo'c'sle as usual.

Tom emerged from quarters. He came out onto the maindeck in the early morning light, blinked, and gazed up at the billowing sails. Then, looking around, he noticed Brod hanging over the starboard side. The great Russian seaman had his work shorts down around his knees and was grasping the ship's rail with both hands. He was defecating into the sea. In proximity to him on the deck was a water bucket and cloth.

Tom had done the same thing countless times now, as there was only one hand-pumped sea toilet on board, in the captain's quarters. He took a turn about the deck. Finding three dead rats lying around, he picked them up by their tails, and threw them one by one into the sea.

A couple of cormorants were flying close by, as if guiding the vessel to land. Suddenly, there was a cry from aloft. Nev's shout was heard loud and clear: 'Land Ahoy!'

Cuttleson took up the brass spyglass he'd placed beside the wheel and extended it. Peering through the lens, he scanned the western horizon, which rose and fell in that strange yet familiar counter rhythm with the vessel. Dead ahead, he perceived the outline of distant islands rising from the sea.

The cook had also heard the shout and came out of the food store to see. He'd developed quite a striking appearance as, during the voyage, he had taken to plaiting his long black silky hair in a pigtail.

Cuttleson continued his sweep with the spyglass. Looking for'ard, past The Wraith and the jib sails, he could now make out the shapes more clearly. There were two land masses, with a wide channel separating them. As they hove into view more clearly still, he called out to the youngster. 'Mister Tom, come up here by me.'

Tom joined him and was handed the spyglass.

'Look there, just off the port bow. You see how that island has smoke rising from inland? That is Mont Pelée. We have reached Martinique.'

The Buccaneer leapt through the waves, heading straight for the channel. The crossing of the Atlantic had been successful.

By early evening, the heroic vessel had doubled the cape at the northern end of the island and had followed its western coastline in a southerly direction. They were within sight of a small bay and the port of Saint-Pierre. The crew went aloft and started reefing sail.

Cuttleson steered her in. As he brought her alongside, the crew threw heaving lines out fore and aft. The quayside workers promptly grabbed hold of them and set about hauling the ship's ropes onto the wharf. They soon had her made fast to bollards.

As the gangplank was being run out, a jolly-looking man, short and with a large paunch that preceded his feet at every step, approached nimbly. This was Monsieur Clot, who held the position and title of Harbourmaster. This honour had similarly been bestowed on his père and grand-père before him. He wore a bright red waistcoat, white flannels and shirt, and blue soft shoes – an outfit that made him appear to all the world as the very tricolor itself. The assemblage was completed by a black shiny kepi worn askew on his head.

In the half-light, M'sieur Clot looked up at The Buccaneer's flag.

'O-ho! Le drapeau de la Grande Bretagne, oui?' he proclaimed, seeming to address the topmast rather than

Cuttleson, who stood at the rail looking slightly bemused by the encounter.

'Eh bien. Combien de temps restez-vous ici?' said the official.

'Um, two…er…deux jours seul. Is it o.k.?… er… C'est bon?'

'Oui, mais comment payez-vous?'

'Nous avons…er…Rum.' Cuttleson thought it wise not to offer too much and added: 'Un cask.'

'Casque?' M'sieur Clot scratched his nose, which was of carmine hue. 'Ah, c'est un fût. Le petit tonneau du Rheum.' (*he pronounced it so*) He stuck his chin out almost as far as his paunch, in contemplation of this offer. He decided after due consideration, that such a payment would indeed be an acceptable tribute to the French State and announced with gusto: 'D'accord! Vive La France!'

Cuttleson called to Tom. 'Fetch a cask of rum up, at the double.'

Tom quickly disappeared, and returned a couple of minutes later, shouldering the cask of spirit. Cuttleson took it from him and brought the rum across the gangplank.

'Fini?' he said to Clot, hoping this would conclude the transaction.

'Oui, très bien. Au revoir.'

Cuttleson gave a quick nod in acknowledgement.

M. Clot perched the cask on one shoulder and carefully did an about turn. Without further ado, he padded nimbly back to the Fees Office, his ample paunch preceding him once again. He reached the doorway, and in fumbling at his waistcoat, dropped the key as he was removing it from his fob-pocket. With the weight of the cask on his shoulder he couldn't do a thing. Moreover, even without the cumbersome yet desirable object, there would have been some doubt as to whether he could bend over far enough to retrieve the key, impeded as he was by his protuberance. Adopting such a posture might result in him rolling over completely, and it simply wouldn't do for a public official to be seen going belly-up.

As the harbourmaster considered this problem, a street boy who happened to be passing and had witnessed the event ran forward and retrieved the key from the ground.

'Merci beaucoup,' said Clot, 'et tu ouvres la porte pour moi?'

The boy inserted the key in the lock and turned it smartly.

Clot proceeded to enter, and put down the cask, while the boy conspicuously continued to hang about by the door.

'Alors, viens ici,' said the harbourmaster. He fished in a pocket of his flannels, produced a five centimes coin and handed it to the child, with the advice: 'Un sou est un sou.' The boy gratefully received his reward and went on his way, whistling.

Aboard ship, Brodnov and Nevsky emerged from quarters after having changed quickly into shore-going clothes. Each carried a hessian sack slung over his shoulder. As they approached the gangplank, Cuttleson accosted them.

'Off out for an evening ashore, eh?'

'Da! Wodka.'

'Well, don't get into any brawls.'

'Aye, sir.'

They went off down the quay to find the nearest bar.

The Wraith had disappeared below decks as soon as the vessel had entered Saint-Pierre bay, and would remain out of sight until she left port. Tom had already turned in, as had Chang. Cuttleson decided he'd do likewise and leave off going ashore until the morning.

Darkness began to envelop the ship. The seventh crew member came on watch and began attending to the task in hand.

The quartermaster went ashore quite early the next day. He needed to replace certain items he'd been unable to locate anywhere aboard. He concluded that the pirates had probably removed them to conceal ashore somewhere for safekeeping. In the Blue Parrot Inn at Port Guardian, possibly. In any case, it didn't matter too much, as he could get hold of the things he wanted, here in Martinique. Saint Pierre was the right place, as it didn't have too many prying eyes.

Saint-Pierre had become something of a backwater since the last eruption of Mont Pelée, which had wreaked havoc on the town at the time. The loss of so many of the beautiful wood-and-stone houses, and the deaths of hundreds of people, had been the greatest tragedy ever visited on the small port. Although the damaged areas were subsequently rebuilt, it was never able to recover its former status, and Fort-de-France further down the coast became designated as the island's capital. There was only a token presence of the Gendarmerie here now.

Cuttleson took to the palm-fringed thoroughfares in the warm air. The beautiful Creole women, with their glistening dark skin, embroidered blouses and cotton skirts, were a joy to behold. A colourful knotted kerchief covered their dark locks. Some of the women were flower-sellers. Each carried a shallow open wooden box balanced on her head, piled high with brightly coloured blooms that wafted delightful scents through the streets. People were shopping in the market, which displayed locally caught seafood, various meats, and spices essential to the Martiniquan cuisine. Coconut milk was a popular refreshment. There was everything one could want for sustenance, and for pleasure eating.

Cuttleson looked about him, then turned into a narrow side alley. He walked a short distance until he came to the open street door of a chandler's premises. Before going in, he glanced back the way he had come, and paused a moment. At the end of the alley, people continued to pass by along the main street. No-one even gave a glance in his direction. Satisfied that he was not being followed, he entered the premises.

The proprietor was checking canvas, cord, lamp oil and other items of stock. He came to the far side of the bare wooden counter. 'Bonjour M'sieur,' he said amiably.

Cuttleson responded with a polite nod, and a short conversation in lowered tones ensued. Two hand-held flags and a jack with a certain motif were the things he desired.

The chandler reached under the counter, where the items were kept concealed, and brought them out. He quoted a price in West Indian francs. His visitor looked at him, and hesitated.

'Problème? Qu'est-ce que vous avez?' said the chandler.

'Acceptez-vous la monnaie anglaise?' replied Cuttleson.

'Mais oui, c'est bon. Pas de problème,' replied the chandler with a shrug. He wrapped the items in paper, tied the parcel up with twine, and handed it over. He knew that his visitor would pay handsomely. Remuneration for a service such as this was quite lucrative.

The transaction thus concluded, Cuttleson left with his purchase tucked under his arm. He had one other place to visit yet, in order to make a few more discreet enquiries.

Chang, meanwhile, was on a tour of the market, accompanied by a porter pulling a wooden trailer. It was already laden with pineapples, bananas, coconuts, cane sugar, sacks of flour, rice, cooking oil, and various other items. The ship's cook was concluding another purchase, of fresh seafood this time. He'd selected crayfish, octopus and crabs, and facilitated his buying spree by signs and pointing, while saying very little. With each of his purchases he offered to pay not with local currency, but with sterling, given to him by the quartermaster, and which he now flourished readily. The market traders, happy for such business to come their way, were quite taken with his assured aspect, his silk garments and pigtailed hair. Once all transactions had been completed, he simply waved the traders away, and beckoned to the porter to follow him back to the ship.

Out on the streets of the small port, the day was getting hotter. Tom, wanting to take in something of the character of this tropical isle, had ventured ashore alone, and had got himself into a situation. A couple of French girls had tagged on to him, trying to importune "le garçon Anglais" to go with them. He was getting a little flustered, as he had no idea how he might shake the young women off. Even the tropical sun seemed to be assisting their enterprise by beating down upon him mercilessly.

Then Fortune lent a hand. Cuttleson happened along, with his recent purchase still under his arm. Seeing Tom's plight, he shouted at the girls as he approached. 'Go away! Allez!'

They looked bewildered at this sudden intervention and became alarmed when he strode up to them and said sternly, 'Il y a un gendarme, proche. Il vient tout près. Allez-vous vite!'

They disappeared smartly.

'Are you all right, Tom?' he asked.

'Y-yes, sir. I… just got a bit lost, that's all,' replied Tom, wiping his forehead.

'Come with me. I'm heading back to the ship anyway.'

They returned to the vessel, which was loading barrels of fresh water.

Later that evening, Brod and Nev came drunkenly along the wharf, shouting in their mother tongue and distracting dockers on a late shift, who were working under rigged lights to discharge the last of the cargo from one of the other ships berthed there.

These two resourceful members of Cuttleson's crew had, for a night and a day, been selling sets of Matryoshka dolls they had carved during the long sea passage. They had then spent a considerable proportion of the proceeds on drink. The local white rum mixed with syrup had soon proved too sweet for their taste, but in one of the several bars they'd visited, they'd had the good fortune to find an enterprising owner who had kept a stock of vodka from the last time a Russian trader had put into port.

If any of the locals working on the wharf in Saint-Pierre could have understood what the two of them were laughing and joking about, they would have known that the rest of the proceeds had been spent on the services of two French prostitutes.

The next day, The Buccaneer put to sea. The crew cast one last glance astern at the Island of Flowers with its smoking volcano, then returned to their work tasks. The ship, under full sail, was heading westward once more; far into the deep waters of the Caribbean, and to what lay ahead.

SEVEN

TRIALS AND PREPARATIONS

Several days had passed since The Buccaneer's departure from Martinique, and the weather conditions had been ever-changing.

An entire day had been spent tacking into a headwind. The next day a strong crosswind prevailed. The next saw the vessel battling against another headwind. Shifting currents added to the difficulties. The ship had been lashed with rain, leaving decks awash. The crew had battened everything down as a precaution in case things got worse still. However, good luck carried them to more settled conditions. The skies cleared, and the vessel was once again running under full sail before a large easterly.

Cuttleson and The Wraith were in the captain's cabin, examining the chart of the Caribbean. The Wraith pointed with a long, bony finger to a position 15°30'N latitude, 71°40'W longitude, far out in the vastness of the sea. The location showed no land marked, but this was clearly the place to which the crew were being directed and must head for. Cuttleson acknowledged and marked it with an "X".

The Wraith withdrew the pointing finger, and drifted silently and coldly through the cabin doorway, out onto the maindeck, then for'ard to take up its station at the bow and resume its westward gaze.

Cuttleson, stroking the rough beard he had now allowed himself to grow, thought for a moment and decided what to do next. He rummaged through lockers and started bringing out an assortment of pirate paraphernalia. There were sashes and bandannas, striped pantaloons and vests, boots, pistol harnesses and various other accoutrements. He spread everything out in the cabin and went onto the maindeck, where he found Brod and Nev by the open hatch, engaged in mending rope. Tom was stationed at the helm.

'Nev! Brod! Leave that and come with me.'

They downed tools and followed the quartermaster back to the cabin.

'Right, men. A change of rig from today. There are clothes enough here to kit out the few of us that there are. Have a look through it all and try things on for size. Go to it.'

The pair set about trying on various items, and before long, they had found all that they needed and had donned the new garb. There they stood, transformed into "men piratical". Even Brod's black bandanna, tied around his bald head, looked the part. So did Nev's choice of a red one, tied about his straggly dark locks.

'The boots as well, Mr. C.? They are not good for work, and will feel too hot,' said Nev.

'Just try some on until you've found a pair to fit you, then leave them in your quarters until they're needed.'

'Aye, sir.'

'Brod. Choose a pair, then relieve Tom at the helm and tell him to come and see me.'

'Aye, sir.'

The two Russian pirates trooped out on deck. Tom, on seeing them, was startled.

'Da! Ha-hah! Looks frighted, eh, dat malchik?' said Brod teasingly. 'Russkiy pirat!' He went up to Tom on the poop, grabbed the wheel and said brusquely, 'Get down to dat cabin an' see Mr. C.!' He was quite ready to clip the lad's ear if he didn't do what he was told, zap.

Tom swiftly disappeared.

'Good day, Mister,' said the quartermaster as the young crewman entered the cabin.

Tom stared at the items scattered about.

'Try some of these things on, and kit yourself out,' said Cuttleson. 'The full rig. I'll leave you to it.' With that, he immediately left the cabin and went to see Chang, who would likewise be needing a change of garb.

Tom selected an outfit comprising a striped vest, a pair of white breeches, and a blue bandanna which he tied in a knot at the back like Brod and Nev had done. He also found a navy blue, close fitted jacket, and decided to wear that. Finally, he managed to find a pair of black boots that were a decent enough fit. He finished putting on his new attire and went out on deck.

'Da, khorosho!' shouted Brod in surprise. 'Privyet, pirat!'

Nev also looked him over and gave a nod of approval. Tom felt pleased at the sudden respect awarded him by the men.

Chang the Chinese Pirate appeared shortly afterwards in his new garb. His shiny black hair was now unplaited and flowed loosely over his shoulders from under a golden bandanna.

Cuttleson himself then appeared, looking equally piratical, sporting a crimson one over his rather unruly locks.

The transformation of The Buccaneer's crew was now complete.

There was a sudden movement at the hatch. Ratter leapt out and padded forward to join the assembled company. She paused to inspect them with her bright, keen eyes. Her long pointed tufty ears were sharply erect.

These features, together with her light mottled fur, revealed her Iberian heritage – that of a Portuguese crossbred lynx. Ratter already had more kills to her name than any of these men. Her seagoing task nearly complete, there was now hardly a rat to be found still alive on this ship.

The Buccaneer sailed onwards, towards her rendezvous with destiny.

A couple of days later, Brod was at the helm when he noticed the sails starting to flap. The vessel's speedy progress began to slow to no more than a few knots. Nev, in the process of checking certain items in the port and starboard deck lockers, also noticed the falling off. Sails began to sag, and soon there wasn't a breath of wind left in them. Clinker's spirit, interrupting its westward fixation, lowered its ghostly head and, gazing down at the waterline, saw that the bow had ceased to cut the waves. The ship and her crew were becalmed!

Ratter, indifferent to such matters, continued to prowl. She followed the starboard rail along the full length of the maindeck and leapt up onto the fo'c'sle. Once there, she sat on her haunches and fixed her gaze on the strange, shimmering figure. She tried to touch the spectre and discovered that her paw went through thin air. She tried sniffing at it. There was nothing but an empty coldness. After a while, she began to lose interest in the curious thing and went off, this time following the portside rail. Paying little heed to Nev, she jumped onto a deck locker, stretched herself up, and began surveying the open water. Dolphins at play had surfaced just a short distance away. They were leaping from the sea, and plunging back in. Again and again they did it, in some kind of joyful game. Curious about such creatures, she became fixated on the spectacle for several minutes.

Cuttleson was in the cabin checking through his log entries. He had taken care that the new log should only provide as much information as suited him, concerning the island to which their journey was taking them. He wanted it to be a record that would not attract too much scrutiny by the maritime authorities. There would be no detailed description of the place itself, nor its location. He made a mental note to erase the "X" marked on the chart once they had found it. Officially they came upon it by chance during their long voyage. After making a few brief notes, he held it to be quite satisfactory.

He locked everything away, and called out to Tom and Chang, both of whom were in the food store. They appeared at the cabin door, and he bade them follow him out on deck.

'All right, men,' he said to the crew. 'We can make good use of this pause. Tom needs experience in close combat. Nev, break out cutlasses from that deck locker.'

Several were brought out. Cuttleson and Tom were handed one each. There followed a lesson in "Parry, swipe, thrust. Disengage. Advance again, swipe left, swipe right".

This went on for some time, the two of them circling and clashing with each other. Tom was occasionally struck by the side of the blade, or lightly touched by the sharp point, which caused him considerable alarm. His apprehension increased further when the quartermaster, having parried a counter-attack, suddenly produced in his free hand a dagger from his sash, and put it to Tom's ribs.

'Guard yourself against that, Mister. Be mindful of it!' said Cuttleson, his nose touching the youth's.

Sweating in the heat, Tom retreated and paused for breath.

The point having been made, Cuttleson also backed off and lowered his weapons. 'All right. Mr. Chang, now you give him a work out.'

'Aiee!' enthused Chang. Adept in armed combat, he embarked on similar routines with Tom, who quickly began to improve. 'He learns fast, Boss!' cried Chang.

Brod and Nev also took up cutlasses. Making space for themselves on the maindeck, they began putting each other to the test, sharpening their already considerable skills.

At this point, Ratter became interested in the commotion and drew nearer to the men, watching them intently.

Nev was stepping backwards under a particularly heavy onslaught from his fellow Russian. He staggered, and in doing so, chanced to spin round. With cutlass still raised, he suddenly found himself facing the lynx.

Ratter's aspect changed dramatically. Spitting, she instantly went into a crouch, poised to launch her own attack.

'Point the blade away!' shouted Cuttleson.

Nev quickly did so, and Ratter immediately recovered her normal demeanour.

Cuttleson, having taken due note of the unexpected development, brought an end to the proceedings, and the cutlasses were stowed. He poured tots of rum for all hands, who gladly sat about, at ease.

Chang then went off to the galley and brought back for the lynx a dish of cold crayfish, and an open container filled with fresh water. She nestled up to him as he stroked her long, pointed ears. He had kept Ratter fed and watered every day like this, from the day she'd been brought aboard at Praia, Cape Verde Islands.

Later that day, with the ship still in the doldrums, Chang cooked a meal for the men.

When chop time was over, three of the crew were summoned to the gun-deck. There, Cuttleson went through the practice of priming, loading, running out cannon, sighting and firing. Then, he made the men repeat, under his timing, the sequence for reloading. He designated Brod as gun-captain, and Tom would give assistance to him and Nev.

Chang was told to be ready to man the swivel gun on the maindeck. The quartermaster himself would steer the fighting ship when the time came. Thus, the preparations were now laid.

Evening came on, and the sky began to darken as the sun dipped below the horizon. The crew, on these warm tropical nights, had taken to sleeping out on deck in thin shorts, and had slung hammocks from stays to bulkheads, or to rigging, or any suitable point they could tie them to. Only the quartermaster remained in a cabin bunk.

By late evening, The Wraith had begun its nightly wanderings; while the lynx, in need of dark diversions, went down into the hold to prowl about in pitch blackness, listening for the movements of any remaining rats on which to pounce with outstretched claws.

The stars appeared once more, and The Buccaneer continued to loll about aimlessly, drifting under a full moon while she waited for the wind to return.

Chang, his long tresses looking silky in the moonlight, lay awake in his hammock long after the others had fallen into their slumbers. He gazed up awhile at the twinkling estrellations, until he too finally succumbed and began to dream of Zhongguo, the Middle Kingdom between Heaven and Earth.

The next morning brought a breath of an easterly. At first, it fluttered the sails falteringly. Then it began to pick up. The Buccaneer, still somewhat askew, responded with a slow roll as if trying to nudge the crew into wakefulness. They were soon up and out of their hammocks and quickly getting a cold wash.

Brod went aft, stationed himself at the helm, and glanced at the compass binnacle. He brought the ship round to point due west again. He had realized too, by the flow of the current, that she had probably been drifting south over the past twenty-four hours. The quartermaster would take more readings today, now that they were under way again, and further course corrections would be needed in order to bring her back onto the desired latitude.

Nev and Tom climbed high in the rigging and began working aloft, unfurling tops'l on both masts. The quartermaster had instructed them to bring all sail into service as soon as the wind strengthened. The vessel felt the favourable conditions, and before long she was surging on again at a high rate of knots.

The Wraith was already at its usual station. Chang went to select some things from the store.

Cuttleson came out on deck in his pirate garb. He looked for'ard, then aft, and noticed that Ratter was right at the stern. She was just emerging from under the raised jollyboat, which had remained unused on this voyage so far. She seemed to be staring fixedly in the direction from which they had come. Brod at the wheel was paying no attention to her.

Cuttleson crossed the poopdeck and came over to Ratter. Following the direction of her unwavering gaze, he glanced at the open sea. Removing the spyglass from his sash, he peered through it and made several careful sweeps of the eastern horizon. There was nothing to be seen, however, apart from the scene he'd looked upon many times over the years. An empty sea under a cloudless sky. Ever since they had got away from the regular shipping lanes and had sailed far from the Windward Isles, they seemed to have had the sea to themselves. If Ratter had seen or sensed something astern of The Buccaneer, there was nothing that he could espy.

Cuttleson turned his attention for'ard again. He knew they could not be far from their objective now and would likely come upon it this very day. He knew the name too, from pirate lore. Those scurvy dogs call it Calico Island. He mused about the number of uncharted hideaways used by the sea robbers. There were rumoured to be more than a dozen around the globe. It was this particular lair, however, that was of interest to him right now.

He returned briefly to the cabin, then reappeared moments later with a set of flags. One of these was a black-and-white standard. He lowered the red ensign on its halyard, replaced it with this, and raised the flag to the masthead. The Wraith at the fo'c'sle turned slowly to witness the skull and crossed cutlasses of a Calico jack. The ship was now flying false colours.

Nev and Tom, noting that the quartermaster had equipped himself today with personal armaments, finished their tasks aloft, came down, and went off to sort out their own items of weaponry. Soon, they had themselves equipped with daggers and cutlasses, and had prepared a full battery of six primed and loaded pistols apiece, in multi-harnesses.

Cuttleson went up to the wheel, grabbed hold of it, and with a stern look at Brod, waved him away with a curt 'Get your weapons ready. You'll be needing them this day.'

At mid-day, Chang in his pirate garb emerged with a large platter bearing a sumptuous meal of crab soup, spicy chicken, a selection of cooked vegetables, and rice. Ratter received the same fare as the men. She licked her lips and disposed of it ravenously while the rest of the crew discussed the action that lay ahead of them. After the meal was cleared away, Chang went to get his own weapons.

In the afternoon, the fair wind that had borne the ship here slackened a little. The vessel slowed and became enveloped by swirls of sea mists. The crew were able to see some distance ahead at one moment, only to find themselves closed in the next. Then they gained a clearer aspect once more. Thus, the mists continued to ebb and flow.

Suddenly, The Wraith raised a skeletal hand again and began pointing. If it did still have Joseph Clinker's heart inside its spiritual being, it must have been fluttering now, in consequence of what had happened the last time the captain was here.

Cuttleson and Nevsky had both noticed a change in the colour of the sea now, which told them they were coming into shallow waters.

'Soundings, Mr. C.?' Nev enquired of the quartermaster.

'Indeed, Nev. Go ahead.'

Nev got the leadline and stood well for'ard. Paying out the plumb end over the starboard side, he started to swing the lead backwards and forwards. Then, at Cuttleson's signal, he threw it ahead of the ship. Carefully watching the line's fathom marker ties, he waited. As the bow came directly over the line, he called out: 'By the mark, Five.'

Tom at the wheel began making frequent small corrections as he kept a watchful eye on the quartermaster's hand signals to him.

Brod went for'ard and made ready to release the anchor. The Wraith had by now removed itself to temporary concealment inside the fo'c'sle head.

The crew could see now, how close to the mystery island they were.

Gathering up slack on the line and feeling the weight on the sandy bottom, Nev called: 'By the mark, Four.'

Cuttleson signalled Brod to standby.

Nev continued to call it. 'By the mark, Three…'

Ratter, appearing from under the jollyboat again, looked about with keen eyes. At a short distance from the shore, she could see a man up on a high bluff. He was observing the ship.

Also noting this, Chang pretended to be casually coiling rope, but in fact was making sure he stayed near the swivel gun in case anyone suddenly appeared on the shore.

Cuttleson, now with a semaphore flag in each hand, raised them both. He carefully spelt out the code he had acquired from paid contacts in Martinique:

D – O – U – B – L – O – O – N – S

The pirate lookout on the bluff, standing out clearly against the sky, signalled with flags back to the ship:

P – A – S – S

The pirate then turned, and slowly disappeared from their sight, behind the bluff.

Nev called out: 'By the mark, Three, less a quarter.'

Cuttleson waved to Brod, who slipped the anchor, which fell with a great splash.

The Buccaneer had arrived at her destination. A thousand leagues had not been in vain. She was now lying at anchor, off Calico Island.

Events were about to take a deadly turn.

EIGHT
ENCOUNTER WITH PIRATES

The quartermaster started rattling out the orders. 'Brod! Get the boat ready. Nev! Give him a hand with the tarp and start freeing those shackles. Chang! Break out two rope ladders over the side. Tom! Lend a hand. Quick as you can, all of you!'

With all possible speed everyone jumped to it. The jollyboat was quickly made ready to be swung out over the stern. The Wraith suddenly reappeared and swiftly installed itself in it.

'Ship's company ready then?' said Cuttleson eagerly.

'Ready!' they cried in unison.

Tom, Brod and Chang climbed in. Ratter leapt in after them. Cuttleson and Nev, remaining on the poopdeck, swung the boat out and lowered it. With a line they brought it round to the ladders. They descended quickly, and stepped in. Casting off immediately, they ran the oars out and two of the crew started to pull, swiftly and silently.

Cuttleson, taking the tiller, steered them towards a point where a copse of trees had grown quite close to the shoreline. This would afford quick cover. On reaching the narrow neck of sandy beach, the bandanna-wearing, armed piraticals stepped ashore and dragged the jollyboat half out of the water. They checked again for readiness their multi-pistol harnesses and bladed weapons, and with The Wraith in the lead, began making their way stealthily through the woods. Ratter stalked alongside them, looking warily about her.

The island had many giant tropical plants, the like of which they had never seen before. They heard the squawks of parrots, and loud calls from unknown creatures hidden in the denser shades.

The Wraith paused and began pointing to something ahead. Cuttleson silently signalled to the others to stop. They listened. They could hear the unmistakable sound of voices not far off. Then, as the group continued their approach with stealth, a house in a glade came into view through the trees. A large group of pirates – perhaps a score of individuals – were present, standing or sitting around, close to the veranda. There were others in the grassy clearing.

The Buccaneer crew moved in silently, while the sleek Ratter, having seen the enemy, crouched low in readiness to pounce, and kept her feline gaze fixed acutely upon them.

Cuttleson drew a flintlock pistol and got the first shot off, bringing down the nearest pirate. The whole group was startled as the crew came at them from nowhere, slashing and stabbing. Ratter leapt towards a leading pirate who had raised a cutlass. She was upon him in a single bound, ripping and biting. The man proved to be no match for the lynx.

The whole scene erupted into a melee of shouting, with cutlasses clashing, pistols going off, and gunpowder smoke filling the air. Chang – who had stopped two pirates in their tracks by getting pistol shots off before his enemies could even prime theirs – stumbled and was about to be run through by a blade, when Ratter suddenly launched herself at his assailant and sank her teeth into the man's neck. Tom, in a clash with another sea-dog, instantly became aware that a dagger had been drawn – the very tactic the quartermaster had warned him about. He swept it aside and swiped at the man, who fell gravely wounded. Brod, giant-like, dragged others to the ground two at a time, and Nev pierced them through.

The scurvy dogs, having been caught unawares, proved to be no match for the crew of The Buccaneer, and soon many lay dead or severely wounded. The remaining few ran for their lives, pursued by Captain Clinker's ghastly-looking spirit, which affrighted them all the more.

Cuttleson himself had suffered a slash wound to the left arm. Chang was also bleeding, from a cut to the forehead. Weapons were scattered everywhere.

'Stay here and keep a lookout, Brod!' shouted Cuttleson. 'The rest of you, follow the Captain!'

Cuttleson proceeded through the open doorway into the house, then paused and looked around warily. At first it seemed that there was no-one inside. Then he saw cowering in a corner a woman, her long raven hair partly obscuring her face.

She swept her hair back and looked up, expecting the intruder to be one of the drunken, brawling pirates come to abuse her again. She did not recognize at first the rough-looking figure standing there, cutlass in hand. Then he spoke her name.

'Morgana!'

She looked again, and gasped. 'Oh, Madre... Is it really you, James?' She clasped her hands together in supplication. Her prayers had finally been answered.

He spoke with urgency. 'There isn't time to explain right now. There are many dangers here yet. We must make haste.'

He glanced around and said, 'Do you have anything that you could carry your belongings in?'

'Sí, and I still have one change of clothes. Just a few things.'

'Gather up whatever you have.'

She quickly began to collect her things and placed them in the large canvas bag she had brought ashore so long ago now. Then she turned to him again. 'Where is my little girl? Where is Fan? I know from the idle talk of los monstruos who stay on this island, that our ship La Madura did manage to get away with some of the crew. My daughter was still on board.'

She paused. 'I am so very weary... Where is my girl, after all this time? Does she live, James? Oh, tell me she lives...'

'She is safe in England. I have cared for her. I will tell you everything as soon as we have got ourselves safely away from here. Come quickly and go along with one of my crew.'

They hurried outside to where Brod was standing guard.

'Brod, take Morgana, and wait by the boat. I have unfinished business here.'

'Aye, sir,' said Brod.

As she and Brod hurried away, Morgana glanced back. Her saviour had already disappeared into the woods.

The quartermaster followed in the same direction that The Wraith and the crew had taken. He had not gone far, when he came upon another scene of recent conflict. Here he found Nev and Tom still brandishing weapons. Several more pirates lay wounded and helpless. The Wraith was close by.

A figure, clearly the pirate captain, was sitting on the ground beneath a tree, with his hands bound. The shoulders of the braided and large-cuffed frock-coat he was still wearing had been pierced by two daggers, pinioning him to the tree. He was bleeding profusely from a deep slash wound to the head, the gore congealing on his face and in his bushy beard. His black tricorn hat, having been knocked off in the struggle, lay on the grass beside him.

What really drew Cuttleson's attention, however, was the area of ground where Nev and Tom were standing. Leaves and branches had been moved, and old ship's timbers had been cast aside, revealing a large cavity below. Cuttleson approached.

'That dog,' said Nev, pointing with his cutlass at the pirate leader, 'and these others you see lying here, were followed to this place. When they saw our Kapitan, they began swiping at the air as he stood before them.'

Cuttleson peered into the cavity and saw a couple of wooden chests. The Buccaneers set about hauling them out. The clasps of the larger one were sprung open first. It revealed a hoard of gold and silver coins, which at first glance appeared to consist mainly of Spanish doubloons and pieces-of-eight. Then, as he ran his fingers through it, he saw that the booty also included later currencies. There were francs, dollars and bundles of banknotes.

Tom and Nev gave whoops of joy at the sight of so much hidden treasure.

'What's in this smaller one?' said Cuttleson.

Nev sprang it open to reveal a cache of drawstring bags and leather pouches. On inspection, the contents of one pouch revealed many beautifully cut diamonds. Others were found to contain rubies, emeralds, sapphires, pearls…

The bleeding pirate captain fumed at the interlopers.

'What to do with him? Kill him, eh?' said Nev, waving the point of the cutlass in the prisoner's face.

'Leave him to his fate, whatever it may be,' replied Cuttleson firmly. 'There will be a few more of his crew still around somewhere. And there has to be a ship here, which must be anchored off the far side of the island. Where is Chang? We need to get away!'

'He disappeared with Ratter, once the fighting had ended,' said Tom.

At that moment, Chang himself reappeared through the trees. He was dragging something bloodied, and Ratter was pacing alongside. It was a wild boar, freshly killed.

'Aiee, Boss! We got fresh pork. Ratter track 'em and bring 'em down. I slit 'em.' He made a gesture, drawing his thumb across his own throat.

Tom looked aghast.

'Bring it,' said Cuttleson. 'Tom, give him a hand to carry that boar.'

Tom grimaced as he and the ship's cook lifted it and took the weight between them.

At this juncture The Wraith approached and hovered by the open pit and treasure chests. Then the strangest thing occurred. It turned slowly to face Cuttleson, and gradually began to fade.

The quartermaster's intuition told him what was happening, and why. He knew what the driving force had been, that had compelled The Wraith to make this voyage. It was atonement. Joseph Clinker's task was now finished. He had made amends to his wife Morgana for the terrible mistake that had ended in tragedy.

'Goodbye, Joe,' said Cuttleson.

The Wraith began to vaporize before their eyes. It gave a final wave of a ghostly hand, in acknowledgement to all shipmates.

A thought came to Cuttleson that seemed appropriate to the moment. It was something he'd once read and now remembered imperfectly: 'Farewell, Spirit. To the elements be free.' He hoped that The Wraith knew his thoughts as it vanished into thin air.

Cuttleson picked up the pirate captain's tricorn hat and threw it into the chest containing the bags of gems. He heaved this up onto his shoulder and held onto it with one hand. With the other, he grabbed one handle of the larger chest. Nev grabbed the other handle. The group trooped off in silence. They were sombre at having witnessed the departure of a fellow crew member, but at the same time they felt elated by their discovery.

Ratter led them back through the woods, and to the beach. As they emerged, they could see that all was well.

Brod was standing guard by the jollyboat, in which Morgana was already seated. Noticing what the group was carrying, the great Russian looked joyful, and hailed them. 'Found da loot! Booty of pirat!'

He threw down his cutlass, clapped his hands in the air, and danced an odd sort of jig.

Cuttleson, approaching with the others, said to Brod, 'Our guiding spirit that brought us here, is no more.' Then he announced to the rest of the crew: 'This is Donna Morgana.'

They heaved the two chests into the boat.

Morgana looked disconcerted as Chang and Tom threw the dead boar in, and she became alarmed when she noticed the cat that accompanied them.

'Oh, James!' She shrank back.

'This is Ratter. She won't harm you,' replied Cuttleson as the lynx leapt aboard. They pushed the boat into the water, and all except Cuttleson clambered aboard. He waded into the sea, pushed the bow out until he was waist deep, and was then hauled aboard by Brod.

'All right! Lay on those oars!' cried Cuttleson from his prone position.

With renewed urgency they began to pull and headed straight for the ship.

As they drew nearer, Morgana looked more closely at The Buccaneer, and exclaimed: 'I am sure this is our ship, La Madura! But she is so changed. Those gun ports. The name is different too… and the flag. I don't understand.'

The jollyboat was brought about as it reached the rope ladders, which were swiftly grabbed hold of. Brod and Nev went up first, then the painter was thrown up to them and made fast. Several ropes were lowered, and the treasure chests were carefully secured and heaved up onto the deck. Next, the canvas bag from the house was brought up. Then Morgana and Tom made the climb.

The ropes were thrown down again. Ratter was secured and hoisted slowly, her legs dangling. Once aboard the vessel and freed from restraints, she looked over the side to see where Chang was. Nev quickly threw the ropes down once more, and the dead boar was dragged up. Lastly, Chang and Cuttleson made the climb, pulled the ladders up and quickly stowed them.

'We can keep the jolly in tow,' suggested Cuttleson. 'All right, men. All hands to the capstan. Lively now!'

'Aye, sir!' came the eager response. The crew inserted the capstan bars, and by laying on with a will, kept it turning until the anchor was raised. Brod secured it. Then, without the necessity of further orders, they immediately began to climb the rigging and set about unfurling sail to get The Buccaneer under way swiftly.

Cuttleson dashed up to the wheel and began to guide the ship out. The crew continued to work up sail as quickly as the situation would allow. Time was of the essence. The vessel began to gather speed quickly.

The seamen came down again. Brod and Nev stowed the treasure chests securely below, and Tom helped Chang to carry the boar into his storeroom to be cut up, salted and barrelled later.

Morgana went to look inside the captain's cabin. Ratter followed her, curious about the newcomer.

Soon they were passing the high bluff again. The sea mists had disappeared in the wind, and as they rounded the headland the crew espied, along the coast, exactly what the quartermaster had anticipated. A ship had come into view from around the other side of the island. She looked to be on a heading that was intended to intercept The Buccaneer and prevent her escape.

'Men to the gun-deck!' shouted Cuttleson.

The gun team went below. Chang stayed on the maindeck by the primed and loaded portside swivel gun. Their respective roles rehearsed during the voyage would all come into play now.

Down on the gun-deck, they set a couple of linstocks smouldering. Tom took one of them up in a bucket to Chang, then hurried below again.

Through the gun port, the team could now see the enemy more clearly. Noting at once that she was a single-masted sloop and more lightly gunned, the two Russians exchanged glances. The significance of this was lost on Tom.

Cuttleson remained at the helm and kept calm. He knew that it would be no use trying to outrun the sloop. She was lighter, easier to manoeuvre, and would overtake the brig. The Buccaneer must stand and fight. He considered the engagement. From his current position, he was still windward of an enemy who was having to tack and therefore had more limited options than he. The Buccaneer could bear down upon them. So, already making good headway, he steered a course to cut across her bow at a notional point ahead.

The pirate sloop was then seen to alter course a little, showing her starboard guns more clearly. A thunderous sound echoed across the water, and a cannonball came whistling through the air. It fell well short. Then came another from a second gun. Short again; but getting closer.

On board The Buccaneer, the gun team had prepared the charge for a chain-shot. Brod staggered under the weight of the two chain-linked cannonballs he'd cradled into his mighty chest with both hands. He accomplished the Herculean task of depositing the projectile in the cannon's mouth. Tom assisted Nev with the carriage tackles. They moved the gun into position and sighted it. Brod signalled to Tom to stand away. Nev paused a moment for the ship to reach the furthest point of the starboard roll, which elevated the port side guns higher still. He put the smouldering linstock to the touch-hole. As the gunpowder ignited, the whole team turned away and covered their ears.

BOOM! The blast from the main charge sent the projectile arcing high over the water. Watching through the gun port, they followed its trajectory. The linked cannonballs seared the air in their deadly flight and began to spin, bolas-like, as they hurtled towards the enemy. The projectile struck with lethal force the sloop's mast at just below half height, shattering it. The direct hit brought mast and rigging crashing down.

The Buccaneer closed rapidly on the stricken ship. Chang could see that the enemy had been ready with grappling hooks to board their opponent's vessel, but now found themselves in complete disarray. There was utter chaos on deck. As no quarter was to be given to these dogs, he blasted them with a full load of grapeshot. The pirates fell like ninepins.

Cuttleson shouted to Chang to come and take the helm, then made a dash for the fo'c'sle head. He had seen a figure in an old reefer jacket and wearing an eye patch, standing on the prow of the sloop. It was Snargel!

Cuttleson gasped as Snargel raised a pistol to him and fired. The ball whizzed close by his head. Without flinching, he drew his primed and loaded long-barrelled flintlock pistol from the harness and carefully cocked it. With arm outstretched, he took careful aim at Snargel, and fired.

The ball hit Snargel dead centre of the forehead. He fell backwards over the far side of the bow and plunged into the sea. As he disappeared into the briny, the soles of his buckled shoes were the last things ever to be seen of him.

The Buccaneer sailed past the crippled sloop.

The battle between the two ships of war had been decisive. Chang turned the wheel and headed out to sea.

NINE

OUR LADY OF SORROWS

A few days had passed. The vessel was heading north under full sail with a fair wind. The false colours had been lowered, and the Ensign raised to its former position. The pirate costumes and weapons had been stowed, and the crew were once again in regular work clothes. They were all going about their various tasks. Except for Ratter, who was stretched out on the hatch cover. She was having a catnap in the warm air.

Cuttleson had removed himself and his personal effects, together with the charts and the ship's log, to the quartermaster's smaller cabin. It was adjacent to the captain's, which he vacated for Morgana herself to occupy, in memory of Joe.

She had suffered such trauma and depredations; it was difficult at first for her to give a full account of the fateful events that had befallen her husband and herself almost a year ago. Then she began to explain how this ship – then bearing the name La Madura – had been contracted by the owner to take a cargo from The Bahamas to Venezuela. This comprised a hundred barrels of sun-dried sea salt, and a hundred and fifty casks of high-quality white rum. The excellent flavour of the Bahamian rum was popular in the bars and restaurants of Caracas, and always fetched a high price.

As ship's captain, Joseph Clinker was able to take his family with him, so she and their daughter Fanny accompanied him on the voyage. He navigated uneventfully, down past the western extremity of Hispaniola, and pressed on, deeper into the Caribbean. Having got halfway across it, cross-currents and strong winds conspired to take La Madura far off her designated course. He found himself in an area of the sea not traversed by him on any of his previous voyages. It was quite by chance that he came upon an island largely hidden by mists.

Clinker decided to go ashore to explore it, and to take several of the crew with him. In order to give his family a spell on dry land after weeks at sea, he also invited Morgana and Fanny to accompany him. Fanny declined, preferring to stay on board rather than venture onto some strange island.

The vessel dropped anchor some distance from the shore, and Morgana joined him in the ship's jollyboat. She was attired in Spanish-style long full skirts and a white cotton blouse with black lace – the same outfit that she was wearing even now. She also took a canvas bag containing some personal items, in case the chance came to bathe in a freshwater pool, and change her clothes too, if she wished.

They stepped ashore, leaving two of the crew by the boat while the rest of the party went off exploring in some woods. She had a fancy they might be able to pick fruit. They had not gone far, when suddenly they were set upon by brigands. She could not believe what was happening. The attack upon them was murderous. Morgana saw several of her companions slain by villains with cutlasses, and she herself was dragged away. Her last glimpse of Joe was seeing him fall while being besieged by assailants. She feared he had been killed or taken prisoner. She never saw him again. She also did not know whether any of the shore party had managed to escape and make it back to the ship.

Cuttleson had listened solemnly to the account given by Morgana. And so, on the second day at sea since the daring rescue from Calico Island, he recounted to her what he knew of subsequent events, as told to him by a mutual acquaintance of theirs in Nassau. A seaman in the shore party had managed to flee the massacre, and reached his fellows waiting by the boat. All three of them made it back to the ship, where they alerted the remaining crew members. Although now short-handed in consequence of the incident, they weighed anchor and set sail immediately. After many deliberations and some argument, they decided to return to The Bahamas to report what had happened.

Young Fanny Clinker was left sobbing in a cabin, having been told by the crew member who had escaped the ambush, that her father had been killed and her mother captured. She spent the entire journey back to Nassau in a daze, wandering forlornly on deck and staring out to sea. A sea that mirrored the emptiness within her.

On that passage home, fights broke out amongst crew members. They were worried that the entire crew might not receive any pay, as they had failed to deliver the cargo. With no proper command, the disputes worsened. One faction wanted to sell the valuable cargo for their own gain, and then disappear. One of the hands stole the ship's log – perhaps with the intention of destroying official records.

Despite the rancour, they did eventually make it back to Nassau, where one of the more responsible members of La Madura's crew delivered young Fanny Clinker into the safe hands of Cuttleson himself, as a family friend and an old shipmate of her father's. Cuttleson and his charge then travelled together to Great Britain as passengers on another ship.

Some months after these events, it was heard in Nassau that La Madura, on a subsequent voyage with a different crew, had got into yet more difficulties in the Atlantic Ocean. Another vessel witnessed, at a distance, the ship being boarded by pirates. After that, she was lost track of completely. That is, until several months later still, a brig named The Buccaneer mysteriously turned up at Port Guardian, the very place that was the quartermaster's home port on the south coast of England.

At the end of the second day of their discussions, Cuttleson conveyed the most difficult news of all to Morgana, regarding the manifestation of The Wraith.

(*It remains unknown how it made its way to England. Perhaps secretly boarding vessels at night-time, as a stowaway? It may forever be a matter of conjecture now that The Wraith has gone. Gone to… Alas no human knows where that undiscovered country is.*)

Morgana became distressed, listless, and anguished by having to take in such information. She began to offer prayers to Our Lady of Sorrows every morning, and every evening, and spent the days alone in her cabin.

From the depths of sorrow, however, hope may spring again. And the thing that was keeping hope alive now, was the knowledge and conviction that she and her daughter would be reunited.

TEN

FLAMENCO

It was some days later. Nev was carrying out the task of checking a bilge pump by the sounding rod, when he found that the water level in the bilge was higher than he expected. He informed the quartermaster.

'What depth is it?' asked Cuttleson.

Nev showed him by the width of his hand.

'Hmm… it isn't too much ingress, considering the length of time we've been at sea.' Then he had second thoughts. 'Well, all right, Nev, we will lighten the ship a bit and keep her stable. Start pumping this one out, and Brod can do the other one.'

They got on with their tasks, and Cuttleson resumed checking the angle of the sun at the noon sight. He concluded that if they could maintain the same rate of progress, they would reach the Mona Passage in another couple of days.

Chang appeared, carrying a large pot, and called

out 'Chop time!' Placing the steaming pot on the hatch, he returned to the galley, then came back again with the bowls and utensils.

Tom lashed the wheel and came down to the maindeck. Brod and Nev joined him, and they sat around enjoying roast pork from the galley woodstove, together with some of the potatoes and onions that Chang still had left in the store.

Ratter presented herself and was given a large chunk from the pot. With her sharp teeth she began to pick carefully at the hot, tasty meat.

Cuttleson went to the captain's cabin and returned with Morgana, who was now sporting shorts and a vest, and had her hair tied back with a yellow ribbon. She was looking well and greeted the men with a cheery 'Hola!'

Chang gave Morgana and Cuttleson generous helpings, then got some for himself.

When most of the crew had nearly finished their repast, Morgana looked at the men and said, 'I have combs and scissors, here in my bag.'

They looked at one another, bemused.

'Well, have you seen yourselves, mis amigos? Your hair is a mess.' She glanced at Brod and laughed. 'Not you, of course.'

Brod merely continued chomping at his meat, as if in a race with Ratter to devour the last morsel.

'Y las barbas,' Morgana added, and elaborated by stroking her own chin teasingly at them.

The crew got the message. The captain's chair was brought out on deck.

Tom went first, so that he could get back to the wheel the sooner. Then one by one they took their turn, including Cuttleson. But not Chang! He would not allow his long, black silken locks to be trimmed at all. However, he did permit Morgana to brush them carefully.

Brod, the last one to submit, sat happily in the chair. It made him feel like a Kapitan. It also pleased him to have his head polished and his beard trimmed.

Morgana then produced a mirror. They all had a good look at themselves and agreed that it was an improvement. With the barber shop session finished, the chair was returned to the cabin.

That afternoon, after studying the charts in his cabin, the neater Cuttleson came out on deck again. On noticing Morgana, he joined her on the fo'c'sle. They stood side by side in silence, looking out to sea awhile.

Then, turning to her, he said 'You are wearing perfume.'

'Sí, Señor,' she replied. After another pause, she added: '– and you like to know why the change in me, James?'

'Yes. Tell me.'

'I have realized a thing importante: Joe would want me to be happy.'

'That is true, and just as it should be,' said Cuttleson quietly.

Feeling more at peace with herself now, she left the fo'c'sle and returned to her cabin.

That evening, Cuttleson suggested that the ship's company hold a celebration, and he offered a whole cask of rum. The crew possessed some musical instruments they had brought with them on joining ship at the start of the voyage. The time was right for a performance!

Also, although they had grown accustomed to being at sea with no ship's lamps lit, so as to avoid being seen by any potential enemies, they decided now in preparation for this evening's event, to light the port and starboard lanterns, and the masthead and stern lamps. In addition, they dressed the ship overall by hanging extra lanterns on the standing rigging of the maindeck.

Brod and Nev brought the balalaikas; and with the ship's sails reflecting the red glow of sunset, they began to sing and play. First in a slow rhythm, then accelerando, they told the story of Katyusha and her soldier lover. Then Nev put down his balalaika, folded his arms and began a Cossack dance. Silhouetted against the great red orb of the setting sun in the west, he began to kick out to the rhythms of Brod's playing.

The assembled company loved the spectacle! Cuttleson, who had been pouring the drinks up to this point, decided in his own merry state that he would have a go at Nev's dance. He made quite a worthy attempt, and was duly praised for his efforts by Brod, who poured him an extra rum afterwards.

Morgana, in long skirts and lace this evening, also had an idea. She went to the cabin, delved into her bag and returned with a set of castanets, and a tambourine which she handed to Tom. In the absence of a Spanish guitar, and being unused to the music of the balalaika, she decided to improvise. Picking up Nev's instrument she was able, with a little ingenuity, to give a quick demonstration of the flamenco style by striking down on the strings with dramatic sweeps of her fingers. Then, handing it back to Nev, she said 'Can you play like that?'

Both he and Brod promptly adopted the Spanish style, and La Doña Morgana began to dance. With arms raised above her head, her raven hair flowing, and castanets clicking, she stamped and rattled her shoe heels loudly on the deck. Making dramatic twists and turns, she swept her long skirts this way and that way as she went round and round the maindeck. It was such a bravura performance from her, not previously witnessed on this voyage.

Ratter, sitting on her haunches next to Chang who was at the helm this evening, turned her tufted ears towards the interesting sounds coming from the lamplit maindeck. She got up and jumped down, and drawing closer, fixed her gaze on Morgana. The dance had stirred memories of her own Iberian ancestry.

The revels went on. There were more songs from the Russians, the rum continued to flow, and a couple of rousing English shanties were sung by Cuttleson.

Eventually, the time came for Nev to take the watch. He relieved Chang, who went straight into the quarters and returned with the ruan – a kind of Chinese mandolin. The entertainment was not quite over yet. He seated himself comfortably on the edge of the covered hatch and began to play. The revellers soon quietened down and gave him their full attention. They became enraptured by the sweet and beautiful cadences of the Orient. Chang played on.

Gradually the hour grew late, and it was time for everyone to turn in. Except Brod, who would soon be taking over the night watch again.

The Buccaneer sailed on in the darkness, in harmony with the sea and wind.

ELEVEN

THE BIRD OF OMEN

Several days ago, when they had reached the 17° parallel, Cuttleson had brought the ship onto a north-easterly bearing. He had continued thereafter to maintain that heading.

When the roistering on the maindeck had finished and another day or so had passed, Cuttleson, with his mind now occupied by a different and impending matter, decided that he must give new orders to the seamen.

'Nev, Brod, I think it prudent to rig stay jacks the length of the ship. Run one out at waist height above the portside decking. Make it as taut as you can, mind you, and then rig another one along the starboard. Also, I want you to prepare safety harnesses, lifelines and shackles. Look sharp about it.' He had observed the sea and sky, felt the wind, and sensed a developing turbulence.

Chang, who had also been given new instructions, was in the galley stowing everything securely.

Tom called out from the helm, 'Do you need me for any other jobs, Mr. C.?'

'Yes, there is one thing. Lash the wheel and follow me. We will try to make sure nothing can break free in the coming hours. It won't take long.'

The two of them went down to the gun-deck and began checking all ordnance, to see that it was adequately secured. Next, they went down into the hold. Everything below was found to be satisfactory, and they returned to the maindeck.

Ratter had resumed her old habit of prowling along one side of the maindeck, and back again along the other.

Morgana was in the captain's cabin, thinking about her daughter.

Although fair weather had lasted for several days, a distinct swell was getting up now, and the increased rolling of the vessel was apparent.

Nev, anticipating they would sight land today, climbed carefully up to the crow's nest.

It was then that the crew spotted the great seabird heading towards the ship with its great wings outstretched.

'What is it, Mr. C.?' asked Tom in surprise.

'That is an albatross,' replied Cuttleson, suddenly looking very solemn. Then he added: 'We must not cause alarm to it in any way.' He almost immediately regretted having said this, but he had been unable to stop himself.

Level-headed and calculating as Cuttleson was, even he wasn't immune from the ancient superstitions of mariners.

The winged creature approached, and as it came overhead, this giant bird of the oceans turned its head, displaying a powerful curved beak and sharp eyes. It looked directly at Nev, and at the ship beneath him. Nev rather foolishly tried to reach out to the creature; it was so close to him. It veered momentarily, then flew on, its shadow passing ominously over the vessel.

Tom had been awestruck at the appearance of the skyglider. As the bird went on its way, his gaze continued to follow its flight, until it eventually disappeared over the south-western horizon. The wandering bird of legend would soar on thermals for a thousand miles, with wings angled for uplift. It was bound for the Isthmus of Panama, and onward to the Pacific.

Sometime later, in the slanting rays of the late afternoon sun, Nev who was still on lookout shaded his eyes, then suddenly pointed and gave a shout: 'Land Ho!' He glanced below him at the quartermaster, who was now manning the helm. The call was acknowledged.

Everyone else had heard it too and came out on deck. Ratter came over to Morgana.

Cuttleson took up the spyglass and extended it. Looking past the edge of the mainsail and jibs, he could make out in the distance the eastern extremity of the land mass that is Hispaniola, rising from the sea. Pleased to have reached here while there was some daylight left, he steered for the strait between the mainland and the tiny Mona islet. He hailed the lookout. 'All right. Better get down on deck, Nev!'

The winds were strengthening now, and the swell was getting higher. The Buccaneer was starting to be pushed around by a force she had encountered many times on her voyages. It was the power of Nature reasserting herself.

'Oh, no! A storm coming!' cried Morgana.

'Shackle the lifelines to your harnesses, men,' said Cuttleson calmly. 'Morgana, take the cat into the quarters and stay there while we ride this out.'

Morgana quickly disappeared, taking Ratter with her.

Cuttleson attached himself to a lifeline. There was no time to shorten sail. It would be too dangerous to attempt it. The storm clouds were gathering rapidly now, darkening the sky.

The ship started pitching as they headed into the Mona Passage. Her bow was riding high on the sea at one moment, then plunging into a trough the next. Then a flash of lightning came, followed by a thunderclap. More followed, and rain began to fall heavily over the storm-tossed vessel. The crew on deck were thrown around repeatedly. The jollyboat astern broke loose from its towrope and was lost. The electrical storm continued to grow in intensity. An ethereal light appeared around the top of the mainmast. It was St. Elmo's Fire! The crew, their uplifted faces shining under the eerie glow, regarded the phenomenon with awe.

Chang in his own safety harness crawled across the deck, dragging his lifeline with him, until he reached the relative safety of the mainmast. He passed a rope around his waist and wound it around the foot of the mast, then took up a sitting position with his back against it. He pulled the rope tight and tied the ends firmly in a reef knot. He then sat calmly, cross-legged and Buddha-like, with his hands open and palms upward, while the elements raged around him.

Chang's oriental features became serene. As serene as those of the prince who sat under the bodhi tree and found Enlightenment.

The Buccaneer was plunging and thrashing about like a wild horse. Small rips were appearing in some of the sails. Nev, Tom and Brod kept a tight grip on the lifelines, clinging to life itself. Inside the captain's cabin, Morgana was on her knees. Hands clasped, she was reciting a prayer: 'Santa María, Madre de Díos.' (*It continues: Pray for us sinners now and at the hour of our death. Amen*)

Cuttleson held tightly onto the wheel. Then he decided to lash it on a heading due north, keeping her bow as close to the wind as he dared, in a desperate effort to get out of the turbulent channel. And then, wanting to check the situation on the maindeck, he let go completely.

That was his one mistake, for at that very moment a towering wave hit. It took him with it, sweeping him across the deck and straight over the rail. Man overboard! He was left dangling over the side, hanging by his lifeline and getting dragged back and forth. With arms and legs wildly thrashing, he crashed into the timbers of the ship's hull again and again as she pitched and rolled. Unable to get back aboard, he began to slip into unconsciousness.

Several of the crew had seen it happen. They struggled across the deck, peered over the side, and saw the quartermaster hanging there, helpless. Nev, with rain lashing his face, signalled to Brod his intention to get to the far stay line. He made his way across – an uphill struggle to negotiate the heaving deck, and then a sudden downhill run, as the vessel lurched again, like a drunken sailor half seas over. He managed to grab hold of a spare lifeline, turn himself around, and struggle back again to Brod, dragging it with him. He shackled him to it, so that his Russian comrade was now held by two lines instead of one.

Another big wave came, threatening to swamp their efforts, but they held on, as Brod took hold of Cuttleson's line and began to pull him up, hand over hand. The quartermaster seemed dead weight, and the great Russian's mighty muscles strained to manage the task.

Slowly but surely, Cuttleson was hoisted to the rail and manhandled over it. Tom and Nev grabbed hold of him by his arms and legs and carried him to the quarters, taking care not to detach either his lifeline or their own, until they were inside. They found the cat hunkered down in the passageway, near the door to Morgana's cabin. Tom shouted, 'Make way there, Ratter,' and she jumped aside. They reached the quartermaster's cabin, carried him in and stripped him of his wet clothes, got him into his bunk, and covered him with a blanket.

Still out on deck, Brod carefully picked his way aft, freed the wheel and got a firm hold on it. Then quite suddenly there came the change of fortune he desperately needed. The heavy rain that had drenched him, began abating almost as swiftly as it had commenced, and the angry doom-laden clouds began to roll away. Although the ship was still pitching in a high sea, there was now sufficient visibility for him to see the cape in the distance on the port quarter. He steered towards it.

The Buccaneer lurched on, and within half an hour she was rounding the headland. Brod continued to lean heavily into the wheel and held her steady until they were out of the Mona Passage, out of the Caribbean, and back in the western Atlantic once more. The courageous ship had run the gauntlet and had made it through to relatively calm waters.

Nature, deciding at last to stand down her marshalled forces of wind and waves, ceased her rebellion.

Tom and Nev reappeared on deck and set about the task of unshackling and stowing lifelines.

Chang, emerging at last from his transcendental state, looked about him and discovered that the up-ended worlds of sea and sky had righted themselves once more. With the planetary sphere now restored to a state of orderliness, he freed himself from the foot of the mainmast, unfastened his harness and lifeline, and handed the tackle to Tom for him to stow it. Then he saw Nev, and asked 'Where is Mr. C.?'

'In his cabin,' Nev replied. 'He went overboard, but we got him back.'

'Aiee!' exclaimed Chang.

'He's taken a battering,' said Tom.

Chang left them hurriedly and went into the accommodation. There he found Morgana watching over the quartermaster, who looked dazed.

'Mr. C. is hurt bad, Moganah?'

'Not so bad as we feared when they carried him in here. I thought he was muerto.'

'I see he is coming round. I check him over. How about you make him hot soup, eh? Maybe we all get some too.'

'Sí, good idea.' She went off to the galley to make it.

Chang pulled Cuttleson's blanket off. He began checking his limbs first. They seemed all right, but the quartermaster winced visibly whenever his shoulders or back were touched. Being suspended above raging seas while thrashing around on the end of a lifeline, was not the best of situations to have got into.

'A survivor, eh?' said Chang encouragingly as Cuttleson realized where he was. 'Lots of bruises, but nothing is broken.'

'Can you help me to sit up?' said Cuttleson hesitantly.

'Sure thing, and Moganah returns soon with a hot soup for you.'

Cuttleson was feeling his bruises.

'I can give you ointment from storeroom to rub on,' said Chang.

'Thank you. You are a man of many parts, Mr. Chang.'

'All same parts as you, Boss,' replied Chang, laughing. 'Better pull shorts up again before Moganah comes back, eh?'

Cuttleson raised a smile for the first time since his terrible ordeal. He managed, slowly and with some difficulty, to sit upright. 'Arrgh! Can you ask Nev to come and see me?'

'I do it right now.' He left to go and tell Nev.

Soon afterwards, Morgana reappeared carrying a steaming bowl of soup on a wooden platter. 'You are sitting up already, sailor!' she exclaimed, passing it to him carefully.

'Thank you kindly. Is everyone else safe?'

'All present and correct,' she replied, giving a mock salute.

He laughed, then winced again on discovering that his ribs were sore too.

Morgana watched him for a few minutes to see that he was managing all right. Satisfied, she returned to the galley and left him in peace.

Just as Cuttleson was finishing his soup, Nev appeared.

'You are looking better already, Mr. C.'

'Thanks to you all, I'm sure I will pull through,' replied Cuttleson. 'Nev, would you take over navigation for a few days, until I'm on my feet? While I am like this, I will spend my time writing up the log and thinking a few things over. You know where we are bound for next. It will take another week, or perhaps less if we have fair weather from now on.'

Nev gave a nod. Then he said, 'While you are sick, some of us will have to take the watch four-hours-on and four-hours-off. Turn and turn about.'

'Hmm… I think Morgana might be able to take one watch, to help with the situation. Just set the course for her and tell her to stay at the helm until she is relieved. And warn all the crew that they must look out for other shipping from now on. Keep a keen eye, Nev. A keen eye on everything.'

'Aye, sir.' Nev left to relay the new orders.

The Buccaneer, by virtue of her own survival, had saved every soul aboard. She was making good headway under clear blue skies once more. She would now continue on a north-westerly bearing, with Nev placed in temporary command. Her destination, The Bahamas.

TWELVE

THE ARCHIPELAGO

The fair weather remained constant. Tom regularly spent hours up in the rigging, out on spars, making minor repairs to sails in situ. Wherever canvas was torn and in reach, he sewed it with cord brought up from the store. He noticed that, on some days when looking down at the rippling sea, enormous green sea turtles would appear and swim away again. To him they were mysterious creatures. Where do the females lay their eggs?

One night, as he lay awake in his bunk, he began thinking about home. He was only fifteen years old when he sailed from Port Guardian a couple of months ago. Now he was past his sixteenth birthday and developing the physique of an adult. He thought about his parents – his father drunk every day; his mother distracted, cleaning when it occurred to her, making meals when she felt like it, and sometimes doing neither. He often had to wash his own clothes. Eventually he'd had enough, so he gathered together a few things, and at the crack of dawn, crept out quietly while his parents were still asleep. He ran away from the house on Fore Street that he had once called home.

He fell asleep at last, knowing that in leaving, he had done the right thing. He would never look back.

A school of porpoise appeared one day, leaping and playing ahead of the bow, matching the ship's speed. Tom, standing on the fo'c'sle head at that moment beside The Wraith, watched them riding the bow wave. He was amazed by their acrobatic display. Ratter became curious as to what Tom was looking at. She leapt up onto a locker, and with her front paws on the rail, stretched her hind legs and looked over it to discover the reason for his fascination.

Tom stroked her head and ruffled her ears. He felt a gentleness inside him towards all the creatures of the world. Also, it was not in his true nature to be fighting pirates, nor fighting anybody. He had made up his mind now as to what he should do; how he might make his way in the world. He resolved to explain his feelings to the quartermaster as soon as possible.

Morgana, stationed at the wheel and maintaining course reliably, kept a watchful eye on the compass binnacle. She liked the fresh sea breeze blowing through her hair. She had taken the helm whenever Nev instructed her to, and she enjoyed being able to help with tasks aboard ship. Each passing day was bringing her nearer to home.

Cuttleson finally reappeared on deck. He felt in better shape now, after his enforced rest. He took a deep breath of sea air, looked about him, and called out. 'Mr. Nevsky! How goes it?'

'Sight by the North Star placed us abeam o' the Grand Turk overnight, Sir. I could see coastal lights to the west. We kept a safe distance from the reefs as we passed by.'

'Not far from the tropic line today then,' affirmed Cuttleson. He looked up at the wind filling the sails. 'And still making good progress, I see.'

'Aye, sir. All north west.'

'Where is Mr. Chang?'

At that moment, the cook himself stuck his head up from the hatchway. 'Been checking the fresh water down below, Mr. C. Two barrels left.'

'Good enough. That will see us through,' said Cuttleson.

Chang went off to get one of the few remaining chickens and wring its neck. He returned with it, sat on the edge of the hatch and began plucking the feathers.

Cuttleson approached the poopdeck, and hailed Morgana. Giving no special favour, he addressed her with the instruction: 'You're relieved, Mister.' Then he called out to Brod, 'Take the helm.' He knew from experience that a swift reassertion of authority after an absence is essential. It is a sure remedy for any slackness that has crept in.

Then he turned to the youngest crewman. 'Tom, I want you to come with me. We will check again below, to see if everything is still as shipshape as it was before the storm. I need to be certain that all gun carriages are still secure, and that we have kept our powder dry. We need to be quite particular about it, after the events on Calico Island. Never take anything for granted.'

The two of them went down to the gun-deck once more. As they were carrying out their inspection, Tom said, 'Mr. C., I need to ask you something.'

'Ask away, Tom.'

'I'd really like to continue my education. You see, I was doing well at school before I ran away from home. I'm good at Geography and Science.'

Halting the inspection, Cuttleson said: 'Sit here, Tom. We must talk.' They seated themselves side by side on a couple of powder kegs. 'You are thinking of higher education, perhaps? What is it that you want to study?'

'Last year we did a project about weather systems, and the continents, and oceans. And marine life. I liked it a lot. The Science of Oceanography, the teacher called it.'

Cuttleson smiled and said, 'Yes. Now I am beginning to understand.' He thought a moment, then asked, 'Where would you like to continue your education? Here in The Americas?'

Tom was taken by surprise. He had not yet thought as to the whereabouts of it, exactly. 'Well, er… yes!' He paused, then looked at the quartermaster rather sadly, and said, '– but I haven't any money. How can I do that?'

Cuttleson leaned forward and said with conviction: 'You are going to be rich, young man! There won't be any problem paying for your education.' He made a gesture, pointing down towards the decking, to those items stowed beneath and out of sight in the hold. 'Down there is kept – well now, how can I put it? Our bank, so to speak.' Then he added triumphantly, 'It is going to be equal shares for all, Mister Tom!'

Tom was left open-mouthed by this revelation.

They completed their inspection of port and starboard guns, the carriage ropes, wadding, cannonballs, gunpowder, etc. Satisfied that everything was in good order, they returned to the maindeck.

Cuttleson cast a glance over the rippling sea. In the near distance he could see ships dotted about, heading here and there among the islands of the Bahamian archipelago. Some were large merchant traders laden with cargoes, others appeared to be small fishing boats.

A little later, Chang called 'Chop time!' He and Morgana appeared, each carrying a large wooden platter. There was a tureen of chicken with five-spice, and plenty of sweetcorn. A big portion was ladled out into a bowl and taken up to Brod, while the rest of the crew sat around the hatch, enjoying the tasty offering. Ratter licked her lips, wolfed it down, and then stretched herself out on the hatch cover for a snooze.

As evening came on, the port and starboard oil lamps in their lanterns were lit. So too, were the white masthead lights on the fore and main, and a stern light. All this was required now, so that other vessels would be able to see The Buccaneer as she entered the regular shipping lanes. In the twilight, Tom routinely took Brod's place at the helm.

Four hours later, when he himself was relieved by Chang, Tom decided to turn in. Lying there in his bunk, he felt pleased with the day's developments. He did not have to return to England. His future lay elsewhere, and his prospects were looking good at last.

The next couple of days passed quickly, with the growing anticipation of their destination. Many of the outlying islets of the archipelago were visible now. A white cottonwool cloud in the bluest of skies hung languorously over each one. Tom, again at the wheel, maintained a distance from them as The Buccaneer passed abeam and left them behind.

Morgana, feeling the gentle roll of the ship, stood at the rail whilst shading her eyes, and watched the islets disappearing astern. She was filled with joy and anticipation now, knowing that they would soon make landfall. She would finally be able to contact her daughter and let her know of the rescue by James Cuttleson. She had previously resigned herself to her own fate, believing she was destined never to leave the accursed place where the drunken crews of pirate ships came and went secretly. Until the day of her salvation, she had no inkling of what had become of the ship, La Madura. And now, nearly a year later here she was aboard her, free again, and sailing home.

The rest of the crew, including Cuttleson, were in a cluster by the opened hatch, gathered around the two treasure chests. They had hauled them up on deck for further examination. Ratter was sprawled nearby, disinterested. The gold doubloons and silver pieces-of-eight shone brilliantly in the afternoon sun. A brilliance that was matched by the gleam in the men's eyes.

'Worth millions roubles!' exclaimed Brod, clapping his hands together.

The others laughed out loud. 'Aye, Brod. It's treasure for all,' said Nev with a grin.

'Aiee!' cried Chang. 'Gold and silver, like Emperor. Ha-haa!'

'Yes, it's quite a haul,' observed Cuttleson. He opened the second chest. He removed the pirate captain's tricorn hat he'd thrown in earlier, and carefully began to take out the drawstring pouches for closer inspection. He noticed one which had a motif of some sort, possibly a Chinese pictograph, sewn onto it. 'Have a look at this, Chang,' he said, passing it to him as he continued rifling through the others.

Chang carefully emptied out its contents. It revealed beautiful rings with finely cut gemstones. There were also exquisitely carved miniature artefacts in green or white jade. 'Imperial quality!' he exclaimed. Then he noticed there was something else in the pouch. Taking it out, he saw that it was a folded piece of paper. When opened, it revealed the vertical writing of Chinese characters. He read carefully through to the end, then gave out a gasp.

Cuttleson, sensing what this might augur beyond their current escapade, looked at Chang. 'Let it remain in your safekeeping from now on,' he said with the prescience he often displayed.

'Aiee!' cried Chang, clutching it to his chest.

They continued to examine the haul, until Cuttleson said to everyone present: 'All right, men, listen up. As you know, we did consider what we might do with a few of these bags before making landfall. And as for the rest, they can be stowed below again with the bullion. All agreed as to the plan, then?' It's time for a final decision on it.'

There was a show of hands, and when the quartermaster hailed Tom and Morgana, they too, each raised a hand. Ratter licked her paws in agreement.

'We are unanimous!' announced Cuttleson. The decision having been confirmed, he took the tricorn hat over to Morgana.

'Would you put this in your canvas bag? There is someone I would like to give this to, after this is all over.'

'Sí, James,' she replied, taking the hat. 'Y muchas gracias, for all that you have done.'

Cuttleson returned to his cabin.

On their last day at sea, they passed scores of cays and some of the larger islands. Finally, The Buccaneer turned and headed for the island of New Providence. She rounded its eastern cape, then followed an outcrop of land known as the Paradise strip, which is separated from its larger neighbour by a narrow strait. On reaching the farthest extremity, she came about and entered the strait itself from the west. They were now in sight of Nassau harbour. Crew went aloft and began reefing tops'l.

A pilot launch came out to meet them. A rope ladder was lowered for the pilot to come aboard.

'Hullo there – Captain?' he hollered.

'Um, I do have command,' said the quartermaster, stepping forward. 'Cuttleson's the name. Come aboard, sir.'

The harbour pilot did so. He shook hands with Cuttleson and waved away the launch.

Under reduced speed now, the ship was guided through the strait. As they drew nearer to Nassau harbour, they could see a section of the Prince George Wharf that was separate from the cargo docks. It was an area where numerous yachts and other sailing vessels rubbed shoulders with cruise liners.

A tug came out to meet her. The tugboat crew were determined to take her in themselves, whether needed or not. The pilot, a good-natured fellow, smiled at their enterprise and allowed them to continue. Their skipper executed a skilled manoeuvre to get in close. 'Holla, there! Lines, if you please.'

Lines were thrown between the two vessels. The tugboat crew were clearly enjoying the reappearance in Nassau of an old sailing ship with gun ports and were making the most of it. The cheers went up as they towed her in. 'Hooray! Hooray!' On arrival, the skipper cast her lines off and nudged the wooden ship into position for berthing. Safely aligned by the wharf, The Buccaneer was promptly secured to bollards. The tug departed with the crew still waving.

The gangplank was run out by Tom and Nev. The pilot gave Cuttleson a final nod and disembarked.

Standing on the maindeck, Cuttleson fixed his attention on a point high above the town. Then he saw it. Unmistakably, he had caught the glint of a telescope mounted on Navigation Hill. He raised a right hand with the palm facing downward and fingertips touching the right side of his forehead. He held the salute briefly; then with a single movement, he brought his hand sharply down and forward with a flourish.

It was done in a style reminiscent, not of the British, as one might have expected from him, but of the United States military. The quartermaster of The Buccaneer had acquired this salutation in a different time and place. It was indeed appropriate now, for the recipient. To that friend and observer who knew him well, its significance was clear enough. It conveyed the hoped-for message: 'We're here. We did it!'

Soon, La Doña Morgana emerged on deck in her long skirts and white cotton top with black lace. As the living embodiment of that southern region of Spain known as Andalusia, she seemed, at this moment, to bring the tide of history once more from Seville to the New World.

Approaching Cuttleson at the gangplank, Morgana swept back her raven hair and said, 'I have to go ashore immediately, James.'

At that very moment, a Cadillac drew up on the quayside, and out of it stepped a tall man whom she and Cuttleson both knew. The man was wearing a white linen suit, open-necked white cotton shirt, two-toned shoes and a Panama hat.

THIRTEEN

NASSAU

Charles Bonnet came aboard, smiling broadly at them. Morgana ran forward. 'Charles!' she exclaimed. 'We meet again!'

'Morgana.' He spoke simply and warmly, with a pronounced American burr. Raising his hat, he kissed her on the cheek. Then he turned to his old friend, Cuttleson. Shaking him warmly by the hand, he said: 'James, I've been scannin' the harbor ev'ry day for weeks now, wonderin' when you might make landfall. This whole darned escapade! If it don't beat all! How *did* you pull it off?'

'There's quite a lot to tell you, Charles,' replied Cuttleson.

Morgana interjected. 'James, Charles. I must leave you both. I have to go ashore to send a telegram to Fanny.' Without another word, she rushed across the gangplank and hurried off along the quay, in the direction of the post office near East Street.

The crew members were all now aloft completing the

furling and tying of sails. The quartermaster had already told them about the owner of the largest shipping company by tonnage in the Bahama Islands. From their vantage points on the yards, they had been looking down with interest on seeing Mr. Bonnet come aboard. He quickly acknowledged them now.

'Well done, guys!' he hollered. They acknowledged with smiles.

Then Ratter suddenly appeared by the hatch. 'And who do we have here then?' he said with surprise.

'This is Ratter, our seventh crew member,' said Cuttleson. 'We found her wandering the waterfront at Praia, Cape Verde.' Then he added, thoughtfully, 'She is in good shape, but I expect we'll be needing a health check and a permit for her here.'

'You will, but I guess there won't be any problem,' said Bonnet. Ratter came and licked his hand approvingly, sensing the importance of the moment. He warmed to her straightaway. 'She will only need a brief quarantine to make sure she's not carryin' diseases. She sure looks fine to me.' He petted her.

The lynx sat on her haunches, looking up at him.

'It's gonna be okay, Ratter,' he said, ruffling her ears.

'Finished here!' came Brod's voice from aloft. 'We can go ashore now, Mr. C.?'

'Of course,' replied Cuttleson.

Brod was first to start making his way down from the yards. Nev, Tom and Chang soon followed.

'And remember, don't –'. Cuttleson was about to continue, but Chang anticipated his next words.

'Get into fights, Mr. C.?'

'Yes, you took the words right out of my mouth, Mr. Chang,' replied Cuttleson.

The four of them went into their quarters to get changed. Bonnet accompanied his friend to the captain's cabin where they sat for some time, as the story of Morgana's rescue and the escape, and a discovery of hidden treasure, was related at length to him.

Bonnet had heard about the spirit of Joseph Clinker – one of his own captains – via Cuttleson's wire from Port Guardian before the expedition set sail. It seemed to him a mariner's yarn at first, and could not have been given credence, were it not for the fact that the message had come from James himself. James, the most level-headed person he had ever met. From the moment he heard about the mysterious brig called "The Buccaneer", he had waited to see if James's suspicion that his missing ship had turned up was true. And it sure was! He was aboard her right now, here in Captain Joe's own cabin. He knew it well enough: the oaken bulkheads, a table right there, and that lamp, and Clinker's own chair in which he himself now sat, listening to James's remarkable account.

This was, without a shadow of a doubt, the lost ship La Madura, the mascot of the Bonnet Shipping Company. She had been transformed into a raider, a ten-gunner, by pirates of the Atlantic! And it was the spirit of a ship's dead captain that had led his friend James Cuttleson to Morgana! He would now have to re-examine his own long-held beliefs in the light of such strange events.

Bonnet also learned now, of the brief but terrifying storm that had almost taken the life of his friend. The crew had come through these trials to bring Morgana home, safe and sound. But why do events like these occur? (*Who or what impels the strange forces that range over the vastness of the oceans? Whose hand is it, that turns the Wheel of Fortune?*)

Their discussions then came around to more earthly considerations. What to do with a hoard of bullion and jewels? The crew had put their own lives at risk in the venture. There had to be ample reward for such bravery.

Finally, Cuttleson told Bonnet of the plan that he and the crew had hit upon. It was a clever scheme. Bonnet liked it and helped his friend to work out how to carry it off successfully.

Nev, Brod, Tom and Chang went ashore with some of the pay that Mr. Bonnet had given them on coming aboard. The group decided to make their first stop at a Turkish Baths they came across in Bay Street, where they could enjoy a spell of luxury after the months of limited comforts. Following this, they went on to other pleasures in West Bay's red-light district.

On board, Bonnet and Cuttleson finalised their scheme which would involve the active participation of the crew themselves when the time came, in order to make it work.

Then they took Ratter directly to the quarantine facility at the wharf.

'Don't worry, bright eyes,' said Bonnet, stroking her head before leaving. 'I'll be back for you, and I'll be bringin' you up to the estate.' As they left, the lynx stared after them, then settled down quietly in her pen to await developments.

On their way back to the ship, Morgana reappeared. She spoke in earnest. 'James! Charles! The International Telegram Service has sent it, to be delivered by messenger to Miss Fanny Clinker, at The Blue Parrot Inn, Port Guardian, Great Britain.' She read out the message she had sent. – MAMA SAFE STOP NASSAU STOP COMING BY SHIP STOP LOVE YOU – 'So she knows at last! Gracias, Santa María!'

'Brava!' they exclaimed.

Then Bonnet had an idea. 'Let's celebrate! Say, how about y'all come up to the big house tomorrow? I keep a small staff there – they will help to arrange food and drink. I'll hire us a band from Downtown.'

'Bueno! I will go shopping for a dress now – and shoes – and a new bag,' said Morgana enthusiastically.

'Bring the ship's company with you tomorrow evenin', James,' said Bonnet.

'I will. That is very kind of you, Charles. Now I want to go and find out what they are getting up to ashore. I'll see you tomorrow then.'

The three characters parted company. The Man in the Panama Hat returned in his car to the house on Navigation Hill. The Spanish Lady took to the boutiques of Bay Street. The Quartermaster followed in the footsteps of his crew. He too, was heading post-haste for the red-light district.

The next morning, Bonnet went directly to Government House. Even in the early part of the day, the air felt warm as he walked to the beautiful pink stucco-finished building which was the residence of the representative Head of State of the Bahama Islands.

Wafting his straw hat to cool his face a little, he paused at the Columbus statue, then began making his way up the stone steps of the portico. Although he had been here on several previous occasions, he was impressed every time he saw those tall, white columns, the vast neoclassical pediment, and the long line of windows with their gleaming white shutters. There was such a reassuring permanence about it all.

As he approached, the great doors of Empire opened before him.

A member of the house staff said quietly, 'Come in, Mr. Bonnet.'

He entered the stately hall, its walls adorned with full-length portraits of past governors of the Crown Colony.

'The Governor is dealing with a matter just now, but I will call you as soon as he's free. Make yourself comfortable.' The assistant promptly disappeared.

Bonnet did indeed feel more comfortable in the cool interior of the building. He began musing about the paintings that surrounded him. The one that always caught his eye was that of Woodes Rogers, the first colonial governor of the Bahama Islands, who put an end to the Pirate Republic of Nassau. It had existed from about 1706 to 1716, a period of significance for Bonnet, because it was around that very time that one of his own ancestors became involved in piracy.

Originally an ex-Militia officer and sugar plantation owner in Barbados, this ancestor had, after some years, inexplicably left his wife and children, bought a sailing ship and hired unemployed seamen from taverns to crew her. He named her "The Revenge", and in 1717 turned to piracy, even collaborating at one stage with the notorious pirate Blackbeard, with whom he established contact while in Nassau.

The "gentleman pirate", as this ancestor came to be called, began to engage in the looting and burning of ships along the American coast. Eventually being apprehended for his criminal activities, he was put on trial in Charles Town (now Charleston), South Carolina, and was convicted of several Acts of Piracy. He received the death sentence for his heinous crimes and was hanged at White Point on 10 December 1718.

Charles Bonnet himself was descended from one of this ancestor's two surviving sons, and that branch of the family had, in due course, moved to Charleston. Several generations on, his grandaddy had started the Bonnet Shipping Company with a single merchant vessel, carrying cargoes between ports on the American mainland and the Bahamian archipelago. As the company grew, the trade expanded to encompass many of the Caribbean states as well.

Bonnet's musings were interrupted by the click of a door opening, and the reappearance of the aide.

'Would you come through now, sir?'

'Thank you.' Bonnet went in. The Governor was at his desk.

'Good morning, Mr. Bonnet,' he said, putting down a sheaf of notes. 'Take a seat. Would you like some tea?'

'Good mornin', Your Excellency. I sure would enjoy some.' He seated himself in an armchair.

Governor Grey gave a nod to the assistant, who promptly disappeared again. Then he got up from his work desk, came over to Bonnet and sat in an armchair beside him. He was glad of the chance to have a break and an informal chat that a visit from the shipping magnate afforded. 'Goodness me, I was astonished when you rang me earlier, Bonnet. What a find! This island that you mentioned… you said it isn't on any charts?'

'That's right. It's a secret hidey-hole where loot was stashed. The bounty of centuries, I believe.'

They both considered this for several moments; two men, each charged with their own responsibilities. Their minds were being exercised by the same thought. Jurisdiction.

The aide reappeared with a silver service, and two fine English bone china teacups and saucers, and some biscuits, all assembled on a large silver tray. He placed it within easy reach and withdrew.

Governor Grey poured. He was a jovial man, known for his playful nature. He quickly spotted an opportunity to play a little joke on his guest. Looking directly at Bonnet, he said flatly and with mock seriousness: 'Garibaldi.' He mischievously enjoyed Bonnet's look of bewilderment for a moment or two, before reaching for the plate and saying to him: 'No, not the military strategist. Have a biscuit. They're really good!'

Then it dawned on Bonnet. This was no talk of campaigns, of military exploits. He'd been had by the Governor again, in another successful ruse!

'Well,' Grey continued, greatly at ease after the coup. 'Your friend – Cuttleson, did you say? – has landed the… loot, in a Crown Colony of H.M. Government. It must be shipped to London for thorough examination by agents of the colonial power.' He considered the matter further while Bonnet continued drinking his tea, and then spoke again. 'Ships of your fleet make the run frequently, don't they?'

'They sure do. The m.v. Providence is loadin' at the cargo port as we speak. If she is ready, she will put to sea sometime tomorrow. And if not, then certainly the day after.'

'I'll send one of our official cars to meet you by the old sailing ship at noon today. Transfer the chests and remind the driver that I said he is to come straight back here with them. I would like to see this hoard for myself before it is shipped. Both chests can then be put securely into a crate for loading.'

'Sure thing. I will see to it, Governor Grey.' They both got up and shook hands.

'Goodbye, Mr. Bonnet. It's been a pleasure to see you again.'

'Thank you, Excellency.'

Bonnet left Government House and headed off in the direction of the waterfront.

The Governor returned to his desk and to other affairs of state.

The Progressive Liberal Party had come to power at the start of the year and had formed the first government to be led by the black people themselves. It represented another great step forward in their epic struggle that had unshackled them from bonds of slavery and brought about Abolition, enfranchisement and other democratic freedoms.

Bonnet walked until he came to the waterfront area. He passed the warehouses, and a recently opened provisions store which was quite busy. Then he noticed a young black boy on the quayside, not far from the sailing ship's berth. He knew the child's name to be Lynden, but he was widely known to proprietors and dock workers as "Rascal." He approached the boy, who was squatting on the ground, and saw that he was playing with coins.

'Hey, Lynden! How's things?'

'Hey, Mr. Bonnet!' the boy replied, looking up at the tall figure. 'I'm checkin'!'

The child had arranged different denominations on the stone quay and was holding a magnet on a string above each coin in turn. After watching him awhile, Bonnet fished in a pocket of his linen suit, and brought out a shiny fifty cents piece.

'Here, check this one for me.'

Lynden took it from him, placed it on the ground and dangled a magnet over it, touching the coin a few times. He gave his verdict.

'It don't pick up. It's good. Means most genwine silver.'

'What else can you tell me?'

The boy examined it further. 'Queen 'Lizabeth II... an' Bahama Islands. Well, dat's us.'

'What's on the other side?'

Lynden turned it over. 'It's a Blue Marlin fish, an' some waves. Der's a date as well – It's last year, 1966.'

'Okay! It's yours to keep.'

The boy gave a broad grin. 'Thanks, Mr. Bonnet.'

'And by the way, shouldn't you be in school today, young scamp? Promise me you'll go directly.'

'Okay, I'm goin' now.'

Gathering up his coins, magnet and string, Lynden stuffed everything into the pockets of his shorts and got up. He went off along the wharf. On reaching the corner of a street that met the quayside, he paused and gave a quick glance back. Mr. Bonnet waved to him. He waved back and hurried on.

Bonnet came to the ship and went aboard.

Cuttleson was already there. He had been aboard the vessel since dawn, having come from The British Colonial Hotel where he and the crew, and Morgana, had all taken rooms for a short stay. On seeing Bonnet, he greeted him. 'Hello, Charles. Did you see the Governor?'

'Sure did. It's just as we expected, James. The chests will be shipped on to the mother country. A car's comin' to remove them to Government House.'

'Right!' Cuttleson was now able to speak with assurance. 'They'll be taken to the British Museum. We can expect a fairly lengthy scrutiny of the hoard.'

The quartermaster and the ship-owner set about removing the hatch covering, threw some ropes down into the hold, then made their way below carefully, one after the other, via the hatchway. They retrieved the two chests from their concealment and Cuttleson made rope slings around each, then he and Bonnet went back up to the maindeck. Putting their backs into the work, they heaved them up. Having accomplished the task, they paused for a breather.

'Phew! What is going to happen to her now, Charles?' said Cuttleson.

'Who? Morgana?'

'No; the ship,' replied Cuttleson. 'She needs an overhaul. I recommend that the old girl be taken to the dry dock facility at Grand Bahama for careening, some re-caulking and re-tarring. Wouldn't you agree?'

The Buccaneer began to sway gently at her moorings.

'Okay, James. It'll be done. Have the crew's personal effects been removed yet?'

'Yes. They've taken all their belongings. Mine went also. They have all gone to the hotel.'

They dragged the chests over to the gangplank. At that moment, a government limousine pulled up. The driver got out and assisted in carrying them onto the wharf and depositing both safely in the trunk.

'Deliver them to Governor Grey at once,' said Bonnet.

'Yes, Sir.'

The car sped off.

'Okay, James,' said Bonnet. 'Let's go and check out the empty quarters.'

They went back aboard and began to look around. Once inside the captain's cabin, they went through every locker. Everything had been cleared as Cuttleson had said. All the pirate apparel that the crew had made use of, had also been taken to the hotel. The galley had been cleared out by Chang. Several other matters had been dealt with too. Cuttleson had passed the ship's new log and the charts to the Port Authority on arrival at Nassau, and he had also been in attendance while the powder kegs were removed into secure warehousing. All cutlasses and large knives had also been handed over, and the pistols had been impounded, notwithstanding the fact that the ship's owner had a firearms licence.

'Well, that all seems okay,' said Bonnet finally. 'I guess I can go and book the band for tonight. I might be able to get The Cool Cats. The caterin' has already been arranged.'

'I'm looking forward to it,' replied Cuttleson.

Bonnet left.

Nev, in swimming shorts for the first time this trip, went for a stroll on Junkanoo beach. He threw off his espadrilles and the T-shirt and waded into the water. A thought struck him. How strange it is, that those whose lives are lived at sea, spend so little of their time actually in it.

Brod also arrived, tramping barefoot through the sand. Then he paddled along the edge of the sea, his big feet splashing as he went. The water was pleasant and cooling.

Morgana had a lie-in, enjoying the luxury of a hotel room. After breakfast, she walked in the hotel gardens, taking in the pleasant surroundings: the yellow elder, the oleanders, the sweet-scented air. Then she thought about her daughter again, and their own future. As far as she could ascertain it.

Tom went for a walk along the bustling, shaded thoroughfare of Bay Street, until he came to a bookstore. He soon found the kind of thing he was looking for. One book, simply titled "The Ocean", had taken his attention. He browsed through its pages. There were photographic plates of amazing sea creatures, corals, aquatic plant life. It also had regional charts of the Earth's seas, their depths, temperatures, and major currents. He made the purchase and headed back to the hotel.

Chang was around Downtown, asking questions of gem dealers.

Cuttleson went over to the wharfinger's office. He arranged for The Buccaneer to be moved from Nassau to the Grand Bahama shipyard for maintenance and signed on Bonnet's behalf to cover the insurance aspects. Then he decided to go and have lunch at the nearby Seagrape Bar. It was a regular haunt of dockers and merchant seamen.

'Ahoy, James,' said one of the sailors as he walked in.

'Hello,' replied Cuttleson. A group of three men were playing a card game. He stood and briefly watched the play of hands. It was the trick-taking game of pinochle.

'Wanna make up a four and play at two-eyes?' said one of them.

'Not just now, thanks. I need a bite to eat, that's all.' He went over to the bar. The bartender, handing him a menu, said 'Here's a list of today's specials.'

Cuttleson studied it. He was feeling quite hungry after the morning's work. He liked the look of Snapper, served in a deep red roux, and decided on it. 'I'll have the fish, please, and some cornbread.'

'Anythin' else?'

'Hmm, let me see. Yes – a side order of pigeon peas with rice.'

'Drink?'

'Just a beer.'

He preferred beer to rum; and was no more interested in the celebrated Bahamian cocktails than he was in the Pina Coladas, Snowballs and Tia Marías on offer in the tavern at Port Guardian in the old country. Drinks for the ladies. Just not his thing. A bar that had beer to sell was sufficient as far as he was concerned.

The bartender served him the beer, then disappeared into the kitchen with the food order.

Cuttleson took his beer to a table outside, overlooking the harbour. Once seated, he gazed across the water awhile, then began to think about the return trip. The m.v. Providence, in common with many ocean-going merchant vessels of the day, could accommodate up to a dozen paying passengers whenever requests were made to the Bonnet Line for passage. Charles would sort out tickets for the group, so that they would not appear as freeloaders to anyone else who might also have booked passage to England on this run.

One of the kitchen staff brought the meal out, a Nassau favourite. Cuttleson savoured the aroma of the fish in tomato, celery and onion sauce wafting up invitingly from his table. 'I'll recommend this to Chang,' he said to himself, as he dipped the cornbread and began munching happily. Such excellent fare!

Later that afternoon, all the ex-Buccaneer companions reassembled at the hotel.

Morgana, whilst on a shopping trip around Nassau, had taken time out to go and see Ratter. She had been informed that the lynx was feeding very well in her temporary captivity, and blood samples had now been taken from her. The results would come through soon, and the vet did not expect to find that the animal was carrying disease. Ratter was still looking healthy and alert. Her fur was sleek. An application by Mr. Bonnet for a permit was likely to be granted.

'They have taken good care of her, James,' said Morgana, 'and I saw how happy she was to see me. Está Bueno! Charles has said there is work for her on the estate.'

'Another job for Ratter? Doing what?' asked Cuttleson, curious.

'La guardia, doing patrol.'

He laughed. 'Ah, guarding the boundary. I like the idea!'

'Haa, better than guard dog, Mr. C.,' said Chang. 'She saved my life on Calico Island.'

'Da! Soldier cat!' exclaimed Brod.

Nev and Tom were amused by the thought too.

'Private Ratter!' said Tom, mimicking a "quick march" up and down.

Cuttleson gave a chuckle. 'Yes! Private, First Class. Just like yourself, Tom.'

Now that they were assembled again, there was one more thing that had to be accomplished today. The crew spent the next half-hour practising their song, which they would be singing later tonight, during the party at the Bonnet residence.

In the early evening, they emerged from The British Colonial Hotel as a group.

Firstly Morgana, in an eye-catching purple strapless evening dress, silver shoes and matching clutch bag. Her hair was swept upwards and decorated with a blue flower. Her nails had been manicured at one of the new salons that were springing up around Nassau. A silver necklace and drop-earrings completed the ensemble.

She was followed by pirates, albeit without weapons now. The whole crew had donned the garb once more, in response to Bonnet's invitation.

It was a balmy evening, and they decided not to bother with taxis. Instead, they went on foot, taking the road towards Navigation Hill. Walking along in their pirate apparel, the group presented quite a spectacle. Motorists who passed by in the twilight flashed their headlamps and gave a toot on the horn.

A policeman, nearing the end of his duty at a crossroads, said: 'Fancy dress party, is it?'

They smiled and nodded, saying nothing.

As they walked on, Cuttleson said quietly to the others, 'If he only knew the things we've done and the places we've been.'

The group had also become aware now, of the considerable number of flying insects that were about at this hour. Bats were also flitting around. They reached a tree-lined stretch of road and Tom suddenly saw, in the gloaming, something of interest that had just alighted on the trunk of a tree, quite close to them.

'What is that?' he said to the others, pointing to where the thing was.

They stopped. It appeared to be a great, furry moth-like creature with frilly antennae. A monster the length of a man's hand from the wrist to the fingertips.

Morgana said, 'I have seen one before with those same grey and brown markings. Some people call it a Bat Moth. Others here have named it the Money Bat; because if you see it, it means you will have riches.' She smiled at the young man. 'Well, you saw it first, Tom!'

Tom took a closer look at the strange creature. As he did so, it seemed to tweak its antennae at him. He could not believe his luck. This had been his best day ever. He had already found a wonderful book about the oceans; and now there was this, the largest moth he had ever seen! He loved this part of the world.

The group moved on, turning into a side road and continuing uphill a little further until they reached the iron gates of the Bonnet estate. These were opened by a member of the house staff, who seemed to be expecting them.

'Hi! Look at you folks! Mr. Bonnet will be pleased. The other guests are inside.' He stepped aside for the group to pass and closed the gates again after them.

They walked up the drive in the still warm evening. The sky had got darker now and the stars were evident. The moon was large, and shone a silvery white.

They passed a parked government limousine and two security men on duty. As the group reached the house, the front door opened. They walked in, to be met by the sound of clinking glasses, soft music, and the buzz of lively conversation. Charles Bonnet was there in his tuxedo, chatting with Governor Grey and others. He broke off from them and came forward.

'Morgana, you look just dazzlin'!'

For a moment they touched as he leaned forward and kissed her on the cheek.

'Dear Charles. What a lovely place this is. So good of you.'

'Guests can choose their drinks at the bar. See over there, where Bindi is? She will help you. No need for formalities. Just mingle. I'll catch up with you again shortly, Morgana.'

She returned his warm smile and took herself away to the bar.

Bonnet turned to the crew. 'Hi, y'all. Say, I like the cut of your jib, James. Bandanna, sash an' all.'

'And you, in your tuxedo, Charles. Let me properly introduce Chang… Brodnov… Nevsky… and last, but not least, Tom.'

'Hi, once again, guys, and welcome.' He shook hands with each in turn, and likewise directed them to the bar.

The other guests had taken note of their arrival. They had been told in advance about Charles's unusual guests and were quite taken up with the whole thing. As soon as the newcomers had got their drinks, they began chatting with them. A young lady made a beeline for Tom.

Morgana was still trying to decide what cocktail to have.

Seeing her there, Governor Grey came over. He spoke without hesitation, his playful bonhomie immediately evident: 'Hello, my dear. I believe you are La Doña Morgana. Bonnet did tell me you were coming along tonight.'

'So pleased to meet you, Governor Grey,' replied Morgana. She offered her hand.

'Please, call me Ralph.' He kissed her hand. 'You are trying to decide on a drink? Might I suggest ... hmm, a Swamp Water.' He relished the phrase.

'Qué?' She gave him a bemused look. 'Really, I couldn't.'

There was a twinkle in his eye as he turned to the waitress. 'Bindi, if you could oblige the lady, I will be forever grateful.'

Bindi had a somewhat mischievous look. 'One swamp water, a-comin' up.' She took a highball glass, half-filled it with ice, poured in a measure of rum, added a dash of blue Curaçao, some orange juice, and a touch of lemon. She deftly stirred the whole thing, and with a flourish served it up to Morgana.

'Muchas gracias, Bindi! Oh, Ralph, it was the cocktail. You teased me!' She broke into laughter.

Governor Grey's latest ruse had worked a treat. He had chalked up another success.

The partygoers sampled a variety of canapés as they circulated. There were also sumptuous dishes on offer. Conch sprinkled with lime juice and spices. Rock lobster – such a delicacy, it simply had to be enjoyed – and sweet-tasting land crabs. There was an abundance of fruits, including guava, mango and sapodilla. It was a Bacchanalia of delights which the house staff themselves could enjoy too, freely encouraged by Bonnet.

After they had consumed this delightful fare, guests were called outside to the terrace, where the band booked for the evening had their instruments and equipment set up.

Charles took Morgana a little farther off to a quieter part of the gardens. They strolled there, chatting beneath the silver moon and the twinkling stars.

It was time for the musical entertainment to begin. The Cool Cats were a five-piece outfit, with drums, guitar, saxophone, trumpet, string bass and assorted extras. The five guys in the band were fronted by a lead vocalist for this gig. As the partygoers made their way to outdoor tables, The Cats struck up with a catchy beat. The singer opened with a firm favourite: "Walk On By". And what a voice she had! There was immediate applause.

When the opening number was finished, she spoke to the audience through the mike.

'Good evening! So glad you did not walk on by… And now, can I just say this to you: 'Don't Make Me Over…'

The applause came again as the band began playing

the intro. The audience were captivated by her sweet, soulful voice.

Next was "What The World Needs Now Is Love". As the show went on, filled with many of those great Bacharach-David compositions, guests got up and started dancing.

The pirate ensemble had their own table. Cuttleson started off with a Sands beer – the same choice that Chang made – and then gave in to temptation with a Jamaica rum. Next, Chang himself began to disappear frequently, only to reappear with a different Bahamian cocktail in his hand each time. Brod staggered off, and returned clutching another bottle of Bourbon, which he had discovered was as much to his taste as vodka. Nev found a bottle of Kentucky sour mash. Tom and his young female companion, Alice, were both drinking the popular coconut water with gin. Then she lured him onto the dance floor to give him some tuition.

The partying continued until late. The singer, having finished her set, sat quietly enjoying a sumptuous meal of rock lobster, spiced salad and cornbread. She had a secret admiration for Charles Bonnet and his many accomplishments.

The Cool Cats, still playing, went into a trad jazz instrumental that took Nev and the now inebriated Brod completely by surprise. The trumpet player, cupping the instrument, did the intro. The drummer followed and the bass began plodding to the beat. The rhythm guitar joined in. Finally, the saxophone began to soar. It was the M. Maturovska-V. Solovyov-Sedoi classic: "Midnight in Moscow"!

Brod, listening with gathering excitement, staggered to

his feet and began stomping to the rhythm: Dah-da-di-dah, da-di-dah-dah-dah. As the beat went around in his head, he went around with it, again and again. Round and round until, inevitably, the terrace started to spin. Within minutes his steering deteriorated, and he went badly off course. He collided with one of the tables, sending bottles and glasses flying. The seated occupants scattered as Brod keeled over and fell with a resounding thud. He was out for the count.

Tom, who had seen it happen, stopped dancing and hurried over to the pirates' table.

'What do we do with him, Mr. C.?'

'Get him upright for a start,' replied Cuttleson, getting up from his seat. 'We can't leave him capsized.'

Nev and Chang just continued to sit there. Neither was keen on the idea of trying to lift the heavyweight Brod from a prone position. Then a couple of guests who had seen Brod's plight came to the aid of Cuttleson and Tom. The four of them managed to haul the great Russian to his feet. He was such dead weight, it took all their strength to hold him upright, but by their best efforts they succeeded in getting him inside and onto a sofa, where he promptly collapsed again.

'Phew! Well, that will have to do,' said Cuttleson. 'I'll ask Charles if we can leave him to sleep it off there until morning.' He looked at the already slumbering Russian. 'He is completely out of it now.'

'Where is Mr. Bonnet anyway?' said Tom.

'I'm not sure. With Morgana somewhere, I expect. We had better get back to the terrace; the band has nearly finished. It's time for our song.'

They went outside again. Already it seemed as if nothing had happened. Many of the partygoers had not even noticed the commotion that had just taken place near their tables.

'It's just as well that Governor Grey could not stay for long tonight,' said Cuttleson. 'It might have been embarrassing for Charles.' He returned to where Chang and Nev were still seated. 'Are the two of you ready, then? Four of us can still do our turn without Brod.'

'Aye, ready now,' the pair replied, getting to their feet at last.

The foursome went over to the stage and stood in front of the band, facing the audience. Two extra stand mikes were put in place as they made ready to sing their song.

They had chosen a song whose origins go way back to the beginning of the 1900s. It has since gone through many changes and has been sung for more than half a century. With the passage of time it has acquired the status of an anthem in The Bahamas. Its story concerns a sponger sloop that Captain John Bethel built in front of his house, near the water's edge. When construction was finished, he and his fellow workers on the project sent her down the slipway. Accompanied by the loud cheering of many onlookers, she was launched at Eleuthera Island.

Local folklore has it, that after some years plying her trade around the Bahamian Islands, and in the Caribbean and several ports along the American mainland, the sloop is thought to have been wrecked, and sank in the early years of the century. Historians still dispute the reason for her demise, and even that a wreck was ever found, but it is certain that she disappeared.

Regarding the words of the song, these may have originally been a poem, later set to music as a shanty. Or a calypso, depending on the style of interpretation, originating perhaps in Jamaica, or elsewhere in the West Indies. It continues to be sung to the present day.

It would be given another lively rendering now by the pirate ensemble. Chang pulled a Chinese bamboo flute from his sash. The band's singer returned to join the extra players on stage and handed Tom a tambourine. She took up her position. The Cool Cats and Buccaneers were ready for the finale.

At that moment, Charles Bonnet and Morgana reappeared. They stood with the audience in keen anticipation of what the augmented outfit filling the stage area could offer them as a closing number. Chang raised the flute to his lips, and in a solo intro, played the opening bars of the tune. The hushed audience held its breath as The Buccaneers began to sing:

'We come out in the sloop John B,
My granddaddy and me,
Around Nassau town we did roam.
Drinkin' all night,
Got into a fight,
I feel so break-up, I want to go home.'
Then came the refrain –
'So hoist up the John B's sails,
See how that mainsail sets,

Send for the Captain ashore and let me go home.
I want to go home,
Oh, let me go home,
I feel so break-up, I want to go home.'

The singer added her own high counter-melody to the refrain. Her soaring vocals echoed throughout the gardens, to the astonishment of Charles and Morgana.

The guitarist in the band, who went by the name of Blake, was from Eleuthera. Recalling his forebear Blind Blake Higgs with his 1930s rendering, he placed the guitar on its stand and picked up the banjo. He always brought it along to the gigs and played it whenever the opportunity presented itself, as it did now.

Nev and Chang leaned into the mike, and continued:

'The First Mate, he got drunk,
He broke into the Captain's trunk,
The Constable had to come and take him away.
Sheriff John Stone,
Why don't you leave me alone?
I feel so break-up, I want to go home.'

Cuttleson, pointing a couple of times at his shipmate Chang for the audience to take note, took the next stanza –

'The Ship's Cook, he took the fits,
He threw away all my grits,
Then he took and ate up all my corn.
I want to go home,

Please let me go home,
This is the worst trip I've ever been on.'

Next came Tom's newly-written stanza –

'Oh, the Quartermaster and me,
We sailed across the deep blue sea,
I ran away, and I won't never ever go home.
I don't want to go home, (Don't make him go home)
Never make me go home, (He ran, ran away to sea)
She is the first ship I have ever been on.'

The audience was really rocking and singing along now. Seeing this, The Cool Cats began speeding up the tempo. The guests excitedly formed a conga chain, which set off through the gardens. Then, weaving in and out of Bonnet's house, they continued singing the refrain at the top of their voices.

The sound of the anthem reverberated from the top of Navigation Hill all the way down to the Prince George Wharf, where the now deserted wooden ship bobbed gently on the tide and began tugging at her moorings, wishing to put to sea once more.

Morgana stayed at Charles Bonnet's house that night. So did Brod, as he continued his slumbers on the sofa. He would have to make his own way back to the hotel in the morning. Tom was given a room by the house staff.

In fact, Tom had been given the run of the house, courtesy of Mr. Bonnet. He had now taken responsibility for the young man's future firmly in his hands at the request of his friend, James Cuttleson.

FOURTEEN
DEPARTURE

It was well after midnight as the remaining trio of Chang, Nev and Cuttleson, having had a marvellous time at Bonnet's party, left to walk back to the hotel. Removing their colourful bandannas now, and stuffing them into their sashes, they made their way off the Bonnet estate. The group retraced their steps down the small side road and soon reached the junction, which was adequately lit. The main road was quiet at this hour, with only an occasional vehicle passing by.

As the three approached the same tree-lined stretch they had walked along just a few hours earlier, Cuttleson caught a glimpse of someone in the shadows. A second glance revealed that there could be more than one. Two, perhaps even three, individuals.

'Nev, Chang,' he whispered, 'I think there might be trouble ahead. Just act casual but be ready in an instant.'

'I see them,' replied Nev quietly.

'Aiee, I see them too,' said Chang.

As they arrived at the spot, three men stepped out directly in front of them. One spoke. He was the biggest.

'Hey, you crazy lookin' guys. Got any dough on you?' His two henchmen gave the group nasty looks.

'Yes, I got plenty,' said Cuttleson. He was outwardly calm, but inside he was like a coiled spring. He quickly registered the fact that the one who had spoken was wearing an earring, with some affectation dangling from it, pierced through the right ear.

The thug laughed and said, 'Hand it over then.' His partners in crime grinned at each other.

Cuttleson, who was facing the man squarely, reached into his own right pocket and drew out a handful of small change. 'Here,' he said to the man. 'Look, you can count it.' He opened his palm to show the few coins in his right hand. Nev and Chang made themselves ready, eyeing the other two men.

The big thug, who had expected more, looked down at the meagre offering. 'Whaa – ?'

Cuttleson instantly threw the coins into the air, and as he did so, quickly reached out with his left hand and grabbed hold of the thug's earring. He gave it a hefty tug, ripping it straight through the man's earlobe. The would-be robber howled with pain. In that same moment, Nev fisted the second one in the mouth, breaking the man's front teeth. The second thug fell like a stone. The third one shot a glance at Chang but was too slow to act. Chang had quickly leaned back as he delivered a swift kung fu kick right in the stomach. The man folded and fell in a heap, clutching himself.

The big man, holding a hand to the side of his head to try and stem the blood, reeled as he took several punches from Cuttleson. He tottered and swayed for a few moments, then fell heavily and ended up sprawled on the ground alongside the others.

Nev and Chang moved to put the boot in, but Cuttleson intervened and pulled them back. 'All right, that's enough. Help me to get them over here, into the trees and out of sight.'

He did not want some passing motorist to stop and investigate before they had a chance to get themselves away from here. He wanted to put some distance between them and the location of this incident.

Urging Nev and Chang to complete the task quickly, he said: 'Let's get it done, and by the time they stagger to their feet again, we will be long gone.'

Without another word being uttered, the three of them set about carrying the villains into the trees, one by one. Getting hold of outstretched arms and legs, they hauled the first one off, then quickly did the same with the second. Finally, they attended to the heaviest thug, who was already returning to semi-consciousness. He kept up a low moaning noise as they dragged him by the feet over the rough ground.

No vehicle had passed during the encounter itself, and the trio of ex-Buccaneers took off smartly. Cuttleson, feeling at his knuckles, said casually to his companions: 'Brod will be annoyed tomorrow, at having missed our latest skirmish.'

'Haa! What you can do with a few cents,' said Chang gleefully.

'Hope they don't spend the money all at once,' said Nev, with a wry smile.

Cuttleson immediately regretted making his last remark, as it encouraged bad thoughts. While it was true that he had no qualms about what had just been meted out, he was at the same time glad that Tom had not been present. After the dangers of the Calico Island raid, he did not want the youngster to be put in harm's way again on his account. His conscience was bothering him.

A little later, arriving back at the hotel in the middle of the night, all three decided to hit the sack and get some much-needed sleep. Earlier at the house party, Bonnet had told them that the m.v. Providence would be leaving on the morrow, at noon. The three of them, plus Brod, and Morgana, would have five passenger cabins placed at their disposal.

The following morning, Morgana, Brod and Tom were dropped off by taxi at The British Colonial hotel.

Morgana immediately changed into a yellow top, white culottes and sandals. An outfit suitable for the balmy weather. A wide-brimmed straw hat provided the finishing touch. She then started packing straightaway, since it would take a little while. Her shopping trips during the stay in Nassau had expanded her wardrobe considerably. She had borrowed two portmanteaux from Charles and would fill them easily from the several shopping bags cluttering the room. She also needed to take the large canvas bag, as that went everywhere with her.

Tom did not take long to change, and he decided to give all his pirate apparel to Morgana as a souvenir if she would accept it. He had no further need of it. He would be able to carry his few remaining possessions and take them with him to Mr. Bonnet's house after they watched the ship leave. He made sure not to leave his Oceans book, and the few items he had brought with him when he first left home.

Brod was still feeling the worse for wear and stamped about his room awhile. He needed to sort himself out, get out of his pirate garb, pack it in his luggage, and put on something more appropriate to his new status as a passenger.

Nev, Chang and Cuttleson had already freshened themselves up and got changed. They were packed, had enjoyed a good breakfast of the delightful Bahamian fare for the last time, had checked out of the hotel, and were now sitting outside in the bright morning. Nev and Chang had their musical instrument cases and a travel bag apiece. Their companion was travelling light.

'Better go and see Ratter before we leave, eh?' suggested Cuttleson.

'Sure thing, Mr. C.,' replied Chang.

'Aye,' said Nev. 'Look, the others are coming out now.'

Morgana, laden with luggage, emerged from the hotel accompanied by Tom. He was carrying a portmanteau as well as his own bag. They were followed by Brod carrying his own musical instrument case and the rest of his luggage.

'Hola!' said Morgana. 'Lovely day to leave for England. I have papers in order, a ticket from Charles, and tickets for you all.' She handed them out to her fellow passengers.

The group made their way to the wharf and went directly to the quarantine facility. As they entered, one of the keepers said to her charge: 'Ratter! Look who has come to see you.'

The lynx pricked up her ears, came forward in her pen and looked at her visitors through the wire mesh. Taking note of the bags they had with them, she looked from one to another of the group. She knew from her days on the Praia waterfront, what it all meant.

Cuttleson was the first to speak. 'It's farewell to you, my lovely,' he said with sadness.

'Bye, Ratter,' said Nev and Brod.

Chang smiled, and ruffled her ears through the mesh. Ratter licked her lips, remembering the crayfish, the chicken and rice, and tasty pork.

'I'll still be around to see you, shipmate,' said Tom kindly.

'I will return,' said Morgana, putting her fingers through for Ratter to nuzzle them.

The group made ready to go, and Cuttleson asked the keeper if she wouldn't mind calling a taxi. They headed for the door, giving Ratter one final wave as they left. They waited outside for a few minutes. A cooling sea breeze was now making its welcome presence felt.

The taxi arrived. It was a London-style, black Hackney cab. Judging by the pristine appearance of it, it must have been exported from Great Britain very recently. Charles Bonnet himself was involved in the importation of the vehicles to The Bahamas. They were proving especially popular with the Nassau tourists, owing to the forward-facing and rear-facing seats that provided plenty of legroom, and enough space to accommodate the copious bags of souvenirs.

'Morgana and Tom,' said Cuttleson. 'When we have got all this luggage in, would the two of you go with it to the cargo docks where the m.v. Providence is berthed? Can you help the driver to deposit everything on the quayside? It'll all be given a quick check over and labelled.'

'Of course, James,' said Morgana.

'Aye, Mr. C.,' replied Tom dutifully.

Everyone helped to load it all in, which left just enough room for the two passengers. Tom and Morgana squeezed in, and the cabbie flicked the meter over, ready to depart.

Cuttleson stuck his head through the open window and said to them both: 'Stay with it on the quayside until we get there, won't you? We don't want anything to go missing.'

'Aye, Mr. C., we won't let it out of our sight,' said Tom.

'Sí, James. Charles is coming to the ship too, to wish me a Buen Viaje, and to collect Tom.'

'Good! See you both shortly then.'

The taxi left.

'We can visit old sailing ship now?' Brod enquired hopefully.

'Certainly, Brod,' replied Cuttleson. 'Let us go and say goodbye to her.' He set off apace, with the others following.

Soon they arrived at The Buccaneer's mooring. She had been stripped of sail now. All the sailcloth had gone to repairers in Nassau, and anything that was too damaged or worn would be replaced. The vessel was ready to be taken under tow by tugs across to the Grand Bahama shipyard. Once she had been towed back again to Nassau, the old ship would be rigged anew. Alas, they would not be here to see it.

The four of them stood on the quayside looking at her. To a man, every crew member began thinking about the extraordinary things that had happened on their long voyage, and the thousands of nautical miles they had sailed in her. Soon their contemplation gave way to emotion. There was a wiping away of salty tears that simply could not be held back. Now it is the parting of the ways.

Cuttleson, feeling the pull in his breast, brought himself to attention. He had felt this before, in another time and place. Raising his right arm stiffly, and keeping the elbow high, he gave the salute.

Seeing this, the others followed suit, one by one, until all four of the brotherhood were at attention. The silence lasted a full minute as a tribute to "the old girl". It was followed by a spontaneous cheer: 'Hooray for The Buccaneer!'

Cuttleson, returning to his normal demeanour, said with finality, 'Well, that's it. We must go.' They trooped off and went straight to the cargo docks. They soon arrived at the m.v. Providence's mooring, where Morgana and Tom were already waiting on the quayside.

The 'P' flag had been hoisted, signifying that the vessel would be departing within the next hour or so. A Bahamian red ensign was flying from the small flagstaff above the bridge, and another fluttered at the sternpost.

All loading was now finished, and hatches had been sealed. The derricks had been swung back into place and made secure for the sea passage. All seamen, and most of the officers, were aboard now. Bosun was directing the hands to the remaining shipboard tasks as they made ready to leave.

The passengers knew that the return trip would be quite different on a motor vessel. Once they were ready to cast off and get under way, the power of her two great diesel engines and twin propellers would churn the sea in their wake. They would transport her across the vast Atlantic in twelve days or so.

Bonnet arrived on the quayside.

'Good morning, Charles,' said Cuttleson.

'Hi, James. There are just a couple of officers yet to arrive and they'll be here soon. Would you all like to go aboard now? All baggage for the passage has been listed, I take it. Your cabins will be ready.'

They each picked out their own luggage, and Tom helped Morgana with hers once again. Quite how she came to have so much did mystify him a little, but he was too polite to say anything.

Bonnet led the party as they went up the steep gangway. He conducted them to the boat deck and into their private accommodation.

The passenger cabins were spacious and looked quite comfortable. Each of the group was invited to choose one to their satisfaction.

Morgana, especially pleased with hers, exclaimed: 'Charles, it is lovely! Gracias.'

'Glad you like it,' he said. 'Now I just need to go up and see the captain, but I will be back real soon, Morgana. I'm not leavin' the ship just yet.'

As soon as he had gone, Morgana's fellow passengers discovered another reason for the quantity of luggage she had accumulated. Every single one of them received a personal visit to their cabin and was handed a surprise package.

'To dress you up a bit!' she announced to each. Quite how she worked out all their sizes, if indeed she had, was a source of astonishment to all of them, but no-one was going to look a gift horse in the mouth.

Charles Bonnet found Captain Ferriday already on the bridge, making ready for the ship's imminent departure.

Ferriday looked distinguished in his tropic whites. They were laundered afresh for the start of each trip, by his lovely wife of forty years. Mrs. Ferriday no longer accompanied him on voyages. She had done so, many years ago, before they had raised a son and two daughters. Nowadays, she preferred to remain at the family home which was situated on the coastal ridge east of Nassau town. She liked to look after the place, keep the garden pretty, and pursue her interest in Art. She could do this to her heart's content.

Ferriday was checking instrument panels and charts.

'Good day, Captain,' said Bonnet cheerily. 'How's things?'

'Hello, Bonnet. My chief engineer ran his test on both engines this morning. We have finished taking on diesel fuel and everything has been running smoothly. First mate and second mate are also back aboard now.' He paused, and from the bridge wing he glanced for'ard, surveying the whole length of the ship.

The owner of the Bonnet Shipping Company knew what was coming next. He liked his older captains, and the readiness for departure would not be complete until the anticipated phrase had been uttered. And it was about to be, right now.

'She's shipshape and Bristol fashion,' announced Ferriday.

Bonnet nodded his acknowledgement and said, 'Have a good trip, Captain.' He quickly returned to the boat deck, where he found Tom looking around.

On seeing him, Tom said: 'I have said my goodbyes to the men, and to Morgana; and I've thanked Mr. C. for all that he has done. I hope to see him again someday. He was like a captain and a father to me.'

'We'll talk some more, Tom, about the continuance of your education, after they have left. I need to say my own goodbyes to James too, and then I want to spend a little time with Morgana before the ship departs.'

'Thanks, Mr. Bonnet,' replied Tom.

Bonnet went to see Cuttleson in his cabin.

'Comfortable enough as a passenger then, James?' he said, smiling.

'Hello again, Charles. Well, it will be quite a change.'

'The two crates were sealed and brought from Government House this mornin', along with diplomatic items and mail,' said Bonnet.

'Good,' said Cuttleson. 'I know how the British Museum does things. It will only keep what is of historical importance. The rest of it will be returned to us. I am certain of it.'

'Sounds okay to me, James!'

'I have explained it to the others. They are in accord, as to where we are going with this. Everyone is willing to bide their time.'

'That's good to hear, for sure,' replied Bonnet.

Neither made any reference to the additional measures they had taken in case any part of their scheme came unstuck. All parties had been sworn to secrecy.

'I want to say thanks for everythin', James' said Bonnet, holding out his hand.

They shook hands. Each knew what the "everything" was. It was something more than financial gain for Charles. As men of the world, they knew from experience that there are other kinds of fortune one may gain in life.

'I must go and see Morgana now,' said Bonnet. 'I reckon it'll be the best part of a month before she's back here in Nassau.'

'Good luck, Charles. And I hope everything works out for Tom as well.'

'I'm quite sure it will, James. That young man will go far.'

Bonnet left Cuttleson examining his gift package from Morgana and called at each of the men's cabins in turn, in order to wish them a happy and safe voyage. Then he came to Morgana's and tapped on the cabin door.

'Por favor, pase,' came the ready response.

He pushed it open. She came to him at once and they kissed.

After a few moments she said, 'Charles, I will see my daughter again.' She paused, then to reassure him she added: 'We will be back here in Nassau very soon.'

'Just get back safely,' he said.

'Sí, but what about you?'

'There are things to occupy me here, as always. The Grants Town and Bains Town developments are comin' along very well. It's a great project, providin' better quality houses for more people, an' that's what's needed.'

'Sí, but I meant, what about yourself?' She knew of his private tragedy of three years ago.

'Don't worry, I'll be fine,' he said. He was more concerned about her than about himself. 'Do you think Fan will really want to return to Nassau? I mean, after the terrible thing that happened to her Pa and to you on that last voyage?'

'Of course, she will want to return!' She held his face in her hands and looked into his eyes. 'The future is here – and Fan will understand.' She kissed him again.

'I must go ashore now, Morgana. I will wave to you when they cast off. The harbor pilot will be here soon. There is just one more passenger yet to arrive, I think. I certainly haven't seen her up here in the accommodation.'

'Oh, I didn't know. Who is she, Charles?'

'Oh, quite an interestin' companion for you and the guys, my dear,' he replied somewhat mysteriously. 'So it's Bon Voyage, Morgana, and a safe return this time!' He turned and left.

He made his way back to the gangway where Tom was waiting for him. A seaman was on standby, ready to haul on the block and tackle to begin raising it as soon as the order was given. Tom and Bonnet went ashore quickly and stood by the quayside.

The harbour pilot appeared, and with a nod to Mr. Bonnet, went aboard and began to make his way up to the bridge.

At that moment, a taxi drew up at the wharf and out stepped the final passenger. She was tall and slender, sporting a white cotton blouse and a knee-length, dark green skirt. She carried a matching green jacket draped over one arm. Under the other arm she kept a large flat box clutched to her side. The box itself looked battered and worn through constant use.

The most striking feature about Caris Meredith, however, was her glorious, flowing red hair. She wore it in tresses down to her waist. It was as if Beatrice Portinari herself had just stepped out of a painting by Dante Gabriel Rossetti of the Pre-Raphaelite Brotherhood, to materialise here at this moment. Caris would even have made the great Dante Alighieri himself swoon.

The cab driver deposited a set of luggage on the quayside, together with what appeared to be an easel. Caris looked around for help, and Tom stepped forward immediately.

'Oh, thank you,' she said, quickly taking stock of the handsome youth. 'I was delayed by all my paraphernalia having to be checked at the gate.'

'Well, you made it just in time, Miss Meredith,' said Bonnet, helping to take the remaining bags. 'The gangway was about to be pulled up this very minute.'

'My mother always said I was born at the last minute, and I've been like that ever since,' she said engagingly.

Caris climbed the gangway with Tom and Bonnet following. They deposited her luggage at the top, where two seamen took over and assisted her up the companionway to the boat deck.

Tom and Bonnet disembarked a second time, and the gangway was then raised. Hawsers were slackened, lifted off the bollards, and winched aboard. Tugs had arrived ahead and astern of the vessel, and they immediately began manoeuvring her away from the quay.

Morgana, Cuttleson and the others came out onto the boat deck and looked over the side. They began waving to the two down on the quay, which quickly began to recede from them. Morgana, waving quite madly now, blew Charles another kiss, and one to Tom.

The harbour pilot, from his vantage point on the bridge, glanced for'ard and aft several times as he maintained contact with the tug skippers on the two-way radios. This continued until the ship was well clear and had been neatly turned, whereupon the tugs departed.

The m.v. Providence, her twin screws churning now, began to move along the strait between New Providence Island and the Paradise strip. She continued until she reached the furthermost western edge of the strip. The pilot launch which had been following her, came alongside and the gangway was partly lowered at sea. The pilot alighted carefully onto the launch as it bobbed about. He touched his cap in a final farewell to the ship and her captain, and the boat sped away back to the harbour.

On the quayside, Tom and Bonnet shaded their eyes and squinted into the distance at the rapidly disappearing vessel. Then they heard the blasts from the ship's whistle, as she gave her farewell to Nassau.

On board, Captain Ferriday looked through his binoculars again and gave the order 'Hard-a-starboard.'

The helmsman turned the wheel and held course under the captain's watchful eye until the ship had completely rounded the headland.

'All right, you can straighten her up now,' said Ferriday. He could relax now that they were heading out. The sea was, after all, his second home. He gave his final order to the officer standing beside him: 'Full Ahead Both.'

The officer receiving his order repeated it and rang the telegraph to the engine-room.

The captain left the bridge.

Soon, the m.v. Providence had cleared land off her starboard beam and began to head farther out towards the wider northeast channel. This would bring her away from the archipelago altogether, and take the ship out into the wider Atlantic, where she would finally set a course east-north-east, bound for Europe.

FIFTEEN

CHARLESTON

A few days had gone by since the departure of the m.v. Providence.

Now that his adventure as a young seaman was over, Tom began to spend several hours each day in the reading rooms situated on one of the upper floors of the Nassau Public Library and Museum.

Surrounded by very tall palm trees and well-kept gardens, it had an imposing structure, designed on an octagonal plan with a colonnade around the top storey, and walls finished in pink stucco. Dating from around the end of the eighteenth century, the building had originally been used as Nassau's first jail. By the 1830s it had ceased to be a place of incarceration and had undergone a major conversion to become a public library and archive. As such, it gradually acquired a large collection of historical documents and maps. In more recent times it had also amassed a considerable quantity of reference books on the flora and fauna of the islands. It also housed numerous nautical charts, and a substantial literature on the diverse species of marine life.

Tom was availing himself of this store of knowledge while Mr. Bonnet continued to make plans for his formal education.

One morning, a member of the staff came up to the reading rooms and informed Tom that a call from Mr. Bonnet had been put through downstairs. He quickly followed the assistant down and picked up the receiver.

'Hey, Tom!' said Mr. Bonnet, 'I received a call this mornin' from Charleston. It's what we've been waitin' to hear, about the school. I'm comin' down from the house now, an' I'll meet you at the wharf.'

'Is it the one you told me about, Mr. Bonnet?'

'Sure is. Oh, an' there's somethin' else as well. Another call came in, directly after that. We can go to collect Ratter!'

'Oh, great!'

'How about if I meet you at the quarantine facility in half an hour, Tom?'

'Right. See you there.'

Tom went back upstairs and put the books and papers away. Then he went outside and took a brief stroll around the gardens to admire the colourful blooms and think about the news. He then left to go and meet Mr. Bonnet.

Arriving at the same time, they went straight in and spoke with the keepers. The two staff on duty informed them that Ratter need not be detained any longer. Tests had confirmed that she was carrying no diseases, and her general health was excellent. Charles Bonnet was asked to sign paperwork to say that he would now be responsible for the lynx on release.

'Do you by any chance have a spare tether?' he asked. 'I don't possess such a thing.'

'Yes, we do. This one should be all right for her,' replied one of the keepers, taking a leather rein and collar down from a hook. She put it around the cat's neck and fastened the buckle. Ratter looked up expectantly at the assistant, and then at Bonnet, and finally at Tom.

'Come on, Ratter. We're out of here,' said Tom, smiling as he grabbed hold of the tether.

He and Mr. Bonnet took the lynx out onto the quayside, where she paused a moment to sniff the air. Then all three set out together. They left the waterfront and headed up to the Bonnet estate.

That evening, as the light was fading, Ratter was taken out on her first sortie by one of the house staff. Starting from the main gates, she padded silently and dutifully alongside him round the entire perimeter, until she found herself back where she started. Then the same exercise was carried out in the reverse direction, finishing at the main gates as before. The task of patrolling an area was an easy one for her. It was not so different from her old habit of prowling about below decks on The Buccaneer, night after night.

When the trial was finished, she was taken to an outbuilding which the staff felt sure would be a suitable place for a cat to sleep. She would have her own quarters from now on. She would soon be allowed to come and go as she pleased, and could venture out to scrutinize anyone or anything, arriving at or departing from the estate.

Bindi came and gave her a feed. She removed the collar and tether. It was an encumbrance, as far as she was concerned, that might only prove necessary in the busy Downtown area. She felt that, after the ignominy of incarceration, Ratter should be able to go about freely, like anyone else.

It was no surprise that Bindi should feel this way. In the early nineteenth century, members of her own ancestral family were amongst those who had been freed from slave ships by the British Navy. They had been chained below decks like animals. Rows and rows of them compacted. Not all survived the appalling disease-ridden conditions and the semi-starvation they were forced to endure. As condemnation of this trade continued to grow, to have been brought instead to The Bahamas among several thousand freed slaves proved a godsend to surviving family members, and to their descendants, who were all able to settle as free people.

Bindi herself had never been to Africa. She was pleased to have Mr. Bonnet as her employer, and she had met Governor Grey on several occasions. Both were such kind men. She felt lucky to have been born in these better times.

❖

The following day, some of Tom's paperwork was sorted out at a government office. For identity confirmation, he had kept the British seaman's card that the quartermaster had obtained for him in England. This and the likelihood of a studentship in the U.S.A. allowed him to be accompanied by Mr. Bonnet as his financial sponsor and guardian.

Charles Bonnet had been quite busy dealing with various matters at his shipping office in Downtown. Those of his fleet that regularly made the sea crossing of a few hundred miles to the American coast were able to make a quick turnaround.

On studying the timetables, the movements and present locations posted on the board by his office staff, he noted that the m.v. Eleuthera, which was currently berthed at Andros and had almost finished loading, was scheduled to make a brief stop at Nassau the very next morning. She would then make the sea crossing to Charleston with her cargo. That would do very nicely. He rang his mother, Cathy.

'Hi, Ma! I will be with you the day after tomorrow, arrivin' on the Eleuthera. Young Tom who I told you about, will be with me. Is it okay for us to stay over with you for one night before visitin' the school?'

'You know it is, Charles,' said Cathy. She had also been informed by her son, of the strange reappearance of the lost sailing ship. And that it was Charles's friend James Cuttleson who found the vessel and brought her home to Nassau.

'After I have taken him there, I'll spend a little more time with you, Ma. There is other important news, which I will tell you about when we arrive. Also, once Tom's affairs have been sorted out, I intend to make a visit to White Point Garden. It's been a while since I was last there.'

'Okay, Charles. Say, how'd you like me to bake your favorite: a tomaytow pie, for when the two of you get here?'

'I sure would!' he replied, laughing. 'It'll be just like old times. I'll see you soon, Ma.'

'I look forward to seeing you, son.'

The next day, Tom, wearing new clothes and carrying his own luggage, said goodbye to Bindi. Then he gave Ratter a big hug. He and Mr. Bonnet promptly left in a taxi. It took them to the cargo docks, where the m.v. Eleuthera was being made ready for departure.

They pulled up at the berth, where her sister ship the m.v. Providence had previously been. She sported the same white funnel with a blue band round the top, and in the centre the British Crown and a banner inscribed BAHAMAS. Between these features there was a representation of an old sailing ship at sea, encircled by a buckled garter inscribed with the legend: EXPULSIS PIRATIS – RESTITUTA COMMERCIA (Pirates Expelled – Commerce Restored).

They went aboard and were met by a steward, who showed Tom a cabin that would be his for the short duration of the crossing. Charles Bonnet went to see the captain with some documents from the shipping office.

The ship was soon out of port and on her way, heading for the north-west Providence Channel. Tom and Mr. Bonnet, standing casually by the lifeboats, and with a fair wind blowing about them, looked out over the stern awhile and watched New Providence Island recede into the distance.

'So, how long is the passage to Charleston?' Tom asked.

'Oh, thirty hours at the most,' his guardian replied. 'The first mate has given the Estimated Time of Arrival as 1800 hours tomorrow.' Then with a smile he added, 'That E.T.A. would be great timin' for Ma's pie!'

A little while later, having emerged from the wide channel, the m.v. Eleuthera turned due north off Florida on longitude 80°W, and headed for the South Carolina coast. There was quite a swell on the sea, but to a vessel of this size and tonnage it was of little consequence, and she continued to make a good rate of knots with engines at full speed.

Tom, unused to remaining in a cabin during the daytime, decided to take a few turns about the boat deck. Pausing at the stern rail, he looked down and watched the frothing of the sea in the ship's wake. The enormous power of a motor vessel's engines astounded him. It seemed a world away from the silent running of The Buccaneer. He turned and went back to his cabin to read his book.

That evening, Charles Bonnet and his young charge dined in the saloon as guests at the captain's table.

The following day was calmer. By the afternoon, the ship had progressed well along the American coast and was drawing nearer to Charleston.

The captain had the bridge. Bonnet hoped there would be no objection to his going up there. Pausing on the companionway, he called out. 'Permission to come up and stand on the bridge wing, Captain? Then I can get a glimpse of the old place again as it comes into view?'

'Come up directly,' came the reply.

Bonnet could see Morris Island on the port quarter and the entrance to the harbour, leading to the point where both the Cooper and the Ashley rivers meet the sea. Engine speed was halved, then cut to slow ahead as they approached a sea buoy. The ship remained there a short while before being guided into one of the cargo terminals for berthing. As she came alongside, the hands threw heaving lines out to dockside workers, who quickly set to hauling the ship's hawsers across. She was made fast and the gangway lowered.

The port of Charleston was busy, as always. Dockside cranes were discharging cargo from ships that came from all over the world. Other vessels were in the process of loading.

Cathy Bonnet was there at the wharf, standing beside the blue Oldsmobile saloon she had driven down in from West Ashley. She waved to her son as he appeared by the top of the gangway with his young charge.

'Hi there, Ma!' hollered Charles. He and Tom made their way quickly down to her.

'You made the crossing in really good time, son,' said Cathy with a welcoming smile. She swept back her now greying hair with one hand and gave him a motherly kiss. Then she turned to his companion. 'So this is Tom! I am pleased to meet you, young man.'

'Pleased to meet you too, Mrs. Bonnet.'

They shook hands. The bags were put in the trunk, and Charles with his young protégé got in the rear seat. Cathy took them straight to the control point.

Soon she was driving them out of the docklands and through the city districts. In one locality, Charles pointed out to Tom the side-yard house on Colonial Street, where his now deceased Pa had spent his own childhood. When Mr. Bonnet Senior had reached adulthood and was newly married to Cathy Silver, the young couple had bought a good-sized house in West Ashley. That was where Charles himself was born, and where they were going now.

Many years had passed by since then, and his Ma was now on her own, continuing to live at the house they had shared. She was happy and quite settled, still enjoying the best of health by God's grace, and still attending Church every Sunday. She had put down roots here, had many friends in the Charleston community and had no desire to be anywhere else.

They drove on and turned west onto Savannah Highway. A few more miles brought them into West Ashley, and to her own neighbourhood. Arriving at the house, Cathy turned into the drive and brought the Oldsmobile to a stop in front of the garage, by the tall trees and beautifully kept lawn.

They got out. Steps led up to a veranda that ran the whole width of the house front. The large windows had white-painted side shutters. Above the main entrance door was a half-circle fanlight in coloured glass, and sidelights etched with a floral motif.

Tom was overawed at first, on seeing a place so grand. It was so different from the house he had known in England!

It was early evening now. Porch lights tripped automatically as they carried their bags indoors.

Cathy Bonnet, accompanied by her son, led Tom through a spacious hall and into a large dining kitchen.

'Would you like to try some of my home-fermented apple wine?' she said proudly.

'Yes, please,' said Tom eagerly. He had never heard of anything like that before.

'Me too,' said Charles drily.

'Well, you don't need to be asked, do you, Charles?' she rejoindered, going to the sideboard.

'That's right, Ma. You know I love it!'

She poured carefully and handed a glass to each.

Charles had also caught the aroma of a tomato pie baking in the oven. 'Just wait till you taste Ma's pie, Tom,' he said proudly. 'Nothin' in Nassau can quite match it.'

The two of them sat at the dining table which Cathy had already set. She brought the steaming dish out with the oven gloves and placed it before them on a wooden platter. Once the pie had cooled a little, she cut two large wedges and served the generous portions to each, and a smaller one for herself. The tang of baked tomato, chopped celery and onions, herbs, cheesy topping and soured cream proved irresistible! They set to with a will. A jug of iced water provided a foil to the delicious, strong flavours.

They soon emptied the plate. Charles and Tom decided to have seconds and helped themselves readily. Cathy looked on with pleasure. It didn't take long for the pair to finish off such a lip-smacking, delicious meal. All that remained was an empty oven dish and a lot of satisfaction. Charles helped his Ma clear the table.

The three then went out into the twilight and seated themselves comfortably in wicker chairs on the porch, to have another glass or two of apple wine. The stars were coming out and a silvery half-disc of a moon shone brightly, suspended in the twinkling sky.

As it was cool outside now, Charles went back indoors and returned a few moments later with a cardigan, which he put around Ma's shoulders.

'So, young man,' said Cathy. 'You're going to see the school with Charles tomorrow morning; and you are greatly looking forward to it, I hear?'

Tom was enthusiastic. 'I am! I can't wait to see it now!'

'That's the spirit, Tom,' said Charles.

The three of them continued chatting about several things, and then Charles and Cathy sat back and listened as Tom gave an account of his adventures on The Buccaneer. She found it a most curious tale. An incredible rescue, and the unlikely story of The Wraith. It was the mention of Ratter, however, that intrigued her the most. Mainly because Charles had already told her that the "adopted" lynx had now taken up residence at his Nassau home.

'Charles! Whatever made you decide to keep a feral cat?' she enquired.

'I don't rightly know, Ma. It just seemed the correct thing to do for her,' said Charles apologetically.

Cathy, in truth, suspected that parts of Tom's story were an elaborate tale worked up to entertain and mystify the listener. A seafarer's fantasy, of course. The hour was getting late, and she showed Tom up to a room that had already been prepared for him.

When she had done that, she decided to make a pot of coffee and bring it out to Charles, to sit with him a little while longer. She worried about him sometimes. The tragic and untimely death of his wife Annie in a road accident three years ago, had been devastating. The loss of Annie had been hard to bear, and it had taken a long time for him to come to terms with it.

They hadn't had any children either, so he did not even have that consolation. Cathy had seen how he threw himself into working with the Bahamian government on the housing projects, as well as continuing to look after his shipping interests. It was work that had kept him going.

Charles began to tell his mother more about Morgana. The way things had developed between them, and how Morgana would also be bringing her own daughter back to Nassau. When this news was given to her, they both lapsed into thought awhile, contemplating the future.

'Okay, I'm off to bed now, Ma,' said Charles after the pause. He felt relieved, now that he had imparted his good news at last. 'Mind if I borrow the car tomorrow?'

'You're welcome,' she said, getting up from her chair. She started clearing the glasses and cups, and they took them inside.

'Good night, Ma,' he said, giving her a kiss on the cheek.

'Good night, son.'

Charles went off to his room, which his Ma always kept spotlessly clean and with a fresh set of linen, in readiness for his visits.

The next morning Tom was up early to prepare himself for one of the most important days of his life. He quickly got himself ready.

After breakfast, he said goodbye to Mrs. Bonnet. Charles took him in the Oldsmobile to Oak Trees, the private boarding college they had been in discussions with.

What presented itself to Tom, as they turned in through the open gates and up the long drive, was an impressive stone building with towers. It looked so different from his school in the small town he had left behind. This school was surrounded, not by narrow streets, but by an expanse of green lawns. He also noticed that it had its own sports fields.

They got out and rang the bell. One of the staff opened the double doors of the main entrance. Bonnet presented Tom and said they had an appointment to see the Principal. The man asked them to follow him. They were taken across what Tom overheard Mr. Bonnet refer to as the quadrangle, and into an oak-panelled study where a distinguished-looking lady was sitting at her desk.

'Hi, Miss Porter!' said Bonnet cheerfully.

'Good morning, Charles! It is so good to see one of the alumni. How are you?'

'I'm very well, thanks, Ma'am.'

Miss Porter had been one of the senior staff during the years he had been at the college. Since that time, she had risen to the position of Principal, following the retirement of her predecessor. They liked continuity at Oak Trees. As a well-respected alma mater, it was not uncommon for one of the old boys to visit them from time to time.

'So this is Tom, from England? How do you do, my young man?' she said with a winning smile.

'Er... very well, thank you, Miss Porter,' replied Tom, feeling slightly nervous now.

Miss Porter asked them to be seated. Getting straight down to business she asked: 'Now, I understand you left England some months ago? Do you have any coursework with you at all, any assignments that you could show to me, from your previous school?'

'Yes, Miss, I still have some of the written work. I brought it with me when I left home.' He produced the schoolwork from his bag and handed it over.

'Thank you. How about some coffee?'

They nodded. Miss Porter picked up the small handbell she kept on her desk and gave it a little shake. At the sound, an assistant promptly appeared.

'A coffee pot for three, please, Maisie. Now, I must take a good look at this.' She put on her half-rimmed reading glasses.

The tray soon appeared, and they helped themselves. They sat in silence awhile and drank their coffee, while Miss Porter continued to peruse Tom's work, some of it extensive.

After several minutes, she peered at him over her glasses. 'Tom, this is quite helpful. It has given me a clear idea of the level at which you have been studying. Charles, this student has missed… what would you say… a couple of months or so?'

'Yes, Ma'am,' replied Bonnet.

'Are you ready to get down to some work if I offer you a place, young man?' she said to Tom. 'There is a lot to be done, you know.'

He nodded and was about to speak, but before he could get the words out, she had already turned her attention once more to his guardian.

'Well now, let me see. You realize of course, Charles, that we are in mid-semester. What the trustees will let me do, is this. I can charge fees pro-rata for the remainder of the current semester, and for the whole of next year's studies as well.'

She gave Bonnet a few moments to consider the commitment involved by both him and the young man. Then, in the absence of any negatives being forthcoming, she rang the bell again without further ado.

Maisie reappeared.

'I would like you to escort this young man over to Miller House,' said Miss Porter briskly. 'He can be lodged there. Tom, go now with Maisie. Welcome to Oak Trees!'

'Thank you, Miss Porter!' replied Tom, jumping up from his chair. He was immediately escorted away. He knew for certain that, from now on, his life would change completely. It would be entirely different from his time spent aboard The Buccaneer, and different again from his previous life with his parents. He felt ready for this.

As soon as they had departed, Miss Porter spoke to Charles again. 'You will also understand that as an international student his stay in the U.S.A. will need to be formalized. I can tell you with confidence that there won't be any difficulty in granting it with you as his guarantor, but we are obliged to submit the correct paperwork, and you and I will go through it now.'

Bonnet felt a sense of relief and accomplishment. He resolved to let his friend James Cuttleson know, as soon as they make contact again, that his protégé now has a place at Oak Trees college, a $7,000 per semester private residential establishment. With the nurturing that Oak Trees provides, Tom can now complete his grades, continue into higher education, embark on a career, and really make something of himself.

Bonnet had also come to an agreement with his own Ma, to have the young man stay with her at the family home in West Ashley during vacations.

When the business with Miss Porter was finished, he went and found Tom in Miller House while the other students were still in their lessons.

'Well, Tom. You have done it! You are a student at my old school, just as we hoped. You have even been assigned to what was my own House group. It will be break time soon, and Miss Porter will introduce you to some of your fellow students. Now she just needs you to add your signature to the forms I have already signed, and then I'll be leavin'. I'll be comin' to see you at Ma's from time to time. You will tell her if there's anythin' you need, won't you?'

Tom was beaming. 'I will, Mr. Bonnet! This is great. It's all thanks to you and Mr. C.'

They returned to the Principal's office, and Tom duly signed.

Charles Bonnet gave his good wishes to Miss Porter. As he went back to the car, she and her new charge came and stood at the main entrance and waved goodbye.

Out on the Savannah Highway, cruising along in the blue Oldsmobile, he felt the joy again of being behind the wheel of the gleaming machine he had bought Ma for her birthday last year. After a while he slowed and turned off down a road which took him back through Charleston's historic district and on to his next destination. He soon reached the memorial park he liked to visit whenever he was in the vicinity.

A light rain started falling as he arrived. He parked and got out, donned the Panama hat and turned up his jacket collar. He walked on into White Point Garden on the Charleston Battery, passing some of the finest statuary on the way. Some of these sculptures commemorated the events and key figures of the Confederacy during the Civil War of 1861-1865, while others commemorated the earlier Revolutionary War of 1775-1783.

He reached the bandstand and admired again the attractive open structure with its tall white columns, which a group of tourists had also come to see. They had got out of their minibus and were enjoying a leisurely walkabout despite the drizzle. He continued along one of the attractively laid oystershell pathways.

The panoramic view of the shoreline was exhilarating. However, this was not what brought him back to the place again and again. It was that memory of the ancestor. The tranquil and leafy aspects of the gardens hid its darker history, and a part of that history would always remain personal to him.

He walked on, and eventually came to the place on the Battery where he always stopped to stare out across the marshes. There was the estuary beyond, where fixed buoys bobbed up and down on the rippling water. They marked the deep channel for the big merchant ships that came and went constantly.

In this location, two and a half centuries ago, executed criminals were left hanging for weeks as their flesh decayed and fell from their bones. One of them was the ancestor, Stede Bonnet. His rotting corpse had eventually been taken down from the gibbet and was buried out on those marshes, beyond the low water mark, in keeping with the practice of the time.

Charles stood in contemplation of this for several minutes, then turned and began to walk slowly along the edge of the parkland. Still deep in thought he tried again, as he always did, to understand what had possessed his notorious ancestor to take up piracy. Some of the historians assert that the retired major from the Barbados militia must have suffered some kind of mental breakdown. No-one would ever really know.

He turned away in silence, and headed back across the memorial park, as rain began falling heavily from a tearful sky.

A couple of days later, the m.v. Eleuthera finished loading another cargo for the return trip to The Bahamas. Cathy Bonnet drove her son down to the docks, where he took his leave of her with a hug and a kiss. He boarded, and within the hour the ship had departed and was soon passing abeam of Fort Sumter in the middle of the channel. He stood at the rail, looking across the water at the old garrison.

When South Carolina seceded from the Union on 20 December 1860, the Federal troops stationed in Charleston withdrew themselves to Fort Sumter. This confounded the new Confederacy, which considered the fort to be the property of the South. In January 1861, the commander for the North, Major R. Anderson, was still holding out. The isolated Federal bastion was surrounded, and a ship with troop reinforcements and supplies, sent by President J. Buchanan, was forced to turn back when it came under fire from Confederate artillery. On 6 April 1861, President A. Lincoln, who had taken office in March, tried again to resupply the fort. On 12 April, General Beauregard, for the Confederacy under President Jefferson Davis, bombarded the garrison for three days, until Major Anderson was finally forced into surrendering.

Rounding the headland of Morris Island, the m.v. Eleuthera turned southward and headed out to sea. On this trip she was bound for Andros with a cargo of machinery, but would first be calling at Grand Bahama, where Charles Bonnet would disembark and visit the ship repair yards to see how far things had progressed. He would take a ferry back to Nassau once he had finished his business there.

During the past week, despite being occupied with many other things, an interesting thought had crossed his mind, concerning the wooden ship. He would consult with shipwrights about a grand conversion of the vessel, and give her a new role, a new existence. It would probably take a couple of months to bring this to fruition and make his latest idea a reality.

The old sailing ship was set to enjoy a different life, based in her home port of Nassau.

SIXTEEN

PASSAGE TO EUROPE

In the first days out from the archipelago, the m.v. Providence passed through an area of the western Atlantic known to seafarers as the Sargasso. Great tangles of seaweed continually drifted by. The ship powered on regardless, until she had passed through it and had left that sea-within-a-sea far behind. There was not much swell to speak of, and the fair weather was expected to continue. The ship was maintaining a north-easterly heading set on autopilot.

Cuttleson, looked every inch the passenger in smart casual wear, and he now sported a light beard that looked trim and better kept. Standing on the boat deck, he looked for'ard and observed the seamen on the maindeck. Many were working along the ship's rail with their chipping hammers, clearing blistered paint away down to the bare metal.

He was familiar with the work. It is to get this done

right around the ship in preparation for the next task, which involves fresh red-leading, to be followed in turn by a fresh top coating of white. As there is not a lot of work for the seamen to do whilst they are deep-sea on one of the world's great oceans, routine maintenance such as this becomes the order of the day. Bosun certainly would not allow them to lapse into idleness. The old adage "the devil makes work for idle hands" is never truer than when it applies to men confined within the bounds of a vessel at sea.

Near to Cuttleson, some of the passengers were lounging about in the deck chairs provided. Brod and Nev were quietly engaged in their favourite pastime of whittling the Matryoshka dolls from blocks of soft wood. Chang was looking on with interest, now that he no longer had the galley to contend with.

Morgana lay sprawled on a towel. She wore a yellow bikini and a wide-brimmed, white floppy hat which shielded her face from the sun. She had just finished covering herself all over in the sun cream bought whilst in Nassau. Having kicked off her sandals, she lay there completely relaxed.

Caris, with her Titian tresses now tied back, was wearing a loose smock with paint daubs all over it, and a soft, peaked cap to give shade to her eyes. She was sitting in the chair she had brought from her cabin. Directly in front of her was the easel she liked to set up after breakfast each day. She had tubes of paints and a set of horsehair brushes to hand, all spread out in the open paintbox on a small table beside her. From these she made various colour mixes on her palette. Working steadily on her canvas, she sat facing the ship's lifeboats, which were suspended from their davits. These were the subjects of interest for her study.

Cuttleson came over to her.

'Hello, Caris,' he ventured. He took a good look at her work-in-progress. Although he had but a passing acquaintance with Art, he did notice the way in which she had exaggerated the shape of the boats. The wooden bows were depicted giant-like in the picture, thrusting forward, towards the observer. There was an emphasis on their being viewed from a low angle. The tall white davits towered threateningly over the boats, and resembled strange birds of prey about to swoop. The white lifeboats were sharply delineated against a pristine, pale blue backdrop.

'I like it,' he remarked. 'I've heard of Surrealism. Is this it? Or am I completely on the wrong tack?'

'Well, James. Let us just say I like to work with unusual shapes. They offer so many possibilities of interpretation.'

'Extraordinary, the way you artists see things.' Not wishing to distract her further from her composition, he added: 'Well, I think I'll take a walk around to the starboard side awhile.'

Caris returned his smile as he took his leave of her, and resumed her concentration.

Brod paused in his woodcarving and asked the others if they would like some drinks. His suggestion was taken up by everyone, and he went off to ask the steward in the small bar by the passenger cabins if he would bring them. Then he returned to his fellow passengers.

Brod, Nev and Chang began chatting about the thing that was always on their minds: the treasure haul. It had been an amazing series of events that had brought them to these present circumstances. They also realized that henceforth, their long-term interests were in common with those of the quartermaster. Of that there was no doubt.

Cuttleson reappeared just as the steward was bringing out the tray of drinks.

'Would you like anything, sir?' the steward asked as he put the tray down.

'Yes, I wouldn't mind a cold beer, thanks,' said Cuttleson, dragging a deck chair into place and sinking into it. Although enforced idleness wasn't really his thing, he was rather enjoying the set of circumstances they were in just now. It gave more time for reflection.

Nev asked the quartermaster directly about the thing they had been discussing. 'How long will your British Museum keep the treasure chests, Mr. C.?'

'No more than a few months I would say, Nev. Not all bullion and gems are of special historical interest. I guarantee that a substantial part of that hoard will be returned to us. I cannot say how much exactly; but trust me, we will get to hear about it through Mr. Bonnet. We came upon it while crewing a ship of his fleet, so they will be obliged to contact him about this affair.'

Cuttleson knew that their discovery was not like the Fishpool Hoard, which had been unearthed by construction workers while preparing a development site in Nottinghamshire, England, the previous year. That hoard comprised mainly fifteenth century English coinage.

'I will be in Leningrad,' said Brod flatly. He took a swig of his vodka.

'And so will I,' said Nev.

'Wherever you may be, just keep in touch with Mr. Bonnet,' said Cuttleson. 'That goes for you too, Chang. He can always be reached through his shipping office in Nassau.'

'Haa, that is good, Mr. C!'

Squalls developed over the next couple of days, and the passengers were forced to stay inside, sheltering from the wet and windy weather. The ship's engines continued pounding away, monitored around the clock by the chief engineer and his dedicated officers of the Bonnet Line.

As their second week at sea commenced, the ship began to display a tendency to stray off course. Buffeted by strong cross-currents and high winds, even a ten thousand tons vessel will count for nothing compared to the powerful forces of Nature. The perpetual movement of such a large body of water, pulled this way and that way by the Moon, becomes an unstoppable force. Human endeavour remains subordinate to that mighty power.

When the turbulence showed no signs of abating, Captain Ferriday had a discussion with the first mate about it. They decided to take the ship off autopilot. Bosun was duly informed, and henceforth he sent a seaman up to man the helm at the start of each officer's watch until further notice. The deck officers continued to order corrections at regular intervals in a concerted effort to keep the m.v. Providence on her designated course.

They were now just over half-way across the north Atlantic and expecting to sight the British coastline in another six days.

As the ship was now coming into distinctly colder latitudes, Ferriday gave the order to all officers to wear Blues as rig of the day.

SEVENTEEN
RESTORATION

On arrival at Grand Bahama, Charles Bonnet went straight to the shipyards and visited the premises of Adams & Co., Shipwrights, who were carrying out the repairs to his vessel. He told the proprietor William Adams about the scheme he now had in mind, and they went to the dry dock to look over the sailing ship again.

Repairs were at an advanced stage. The exposed hull had been careened, and hot pitch had been freshly added between timbers throughout. The rudder assembly appeared to be still in perfectly good order.

The craftsmen and labourers were on their break. Bonnet, with a greeting to them, clambered up onto the ship's maindeck via one of the workmen's ladders, with Adams following.

Bonnet conducted him straight to the gun-deck. The plan, he explained to the shipwright, was to have all guns removed except for a single cannon, and to have the emptied gun-deck fitted out as a restaurant, with a well-equipped kitchen for the chefs, a well-stocked bar, and toilet amenities for the diners. Most of the existing gun ports could be converted into windows. Adams began busily taking measurements and making notes as they discussed in detail what could go where.

Next, they went down into the hold, which had workmen's temporary cluster lights rigged up on electric cables. Stepping carefully, they inspected it. All parts of it, and particularly the bilges, were still in the process of being thoroughly cleaned and disinfected as Bonnet had instructed. He suggested to Adams that this part of the ship could house the generators, and refrigerators, and still have plenty of space left for equipment storage.

Going back up to the maindeck, they examined it thoroughly. Bonnet noted that the re-caulking had been completed. Then they moved on into the accommodation aft.

'There will be new crew quarters here,' said Bonnet. 'The vessel will be kept seaworthy and fully rigged so we can continue to sail her around the islands from time to time. I suggest also, Mr. Adams, that besides havin' electric lightin' for the restaurant, the kitchen, etcetera, the old oil lamps can also be replaced by modern navigation lights. What do you reckon, then?' The more he talked about it, the more excited he began to feel about the whole thing, but he still needed approval by the expert.

'Certainly, Mr. Bonnet. I can have an extra team taken on for the whole project, to work alongside the carpenters.'

Adams paused a moment. 'I do suggest though, ye should keep the old oil lamps as a back-up. Don't discard 'em.'

'That's a good point!' replied Bonnet. 'I'm grateful for the advice.'

'And where are things up to with the sails?' asked Adams, looking up at the masts and the bare yards.

'Sailmakers in Nassau have just been in touch. All sailcloth has been checked now for wear, and I have agreed their estimate for repairs and replacement. A rigging team will re-hang the sails.'

'It's an ambitious project, Mr. Bonnet!' said Adams. 'I'll be pleased to help see it through to completion, o' course.'

'I feel an obligation to do right by the old girl. She is the company mascot, after all. And will remain so after this, even though she's taken her last deep-sea voyage. I'll see her right.'

'Well, I hope I may dine aboard her once she's shipshape again!'

'You can be sure you'll be one of the first guests invited aboard for a slap-up meal in the newest floatin' restaurant in Nassau. Just as soon as it opens for business, Mr. Adams!'

'Thank ye kindly, Mr. Bonnet.'

The two men shook hands on it.

They returned to Adams's premises where they worked out costings for each phase of the new project. During this important and detailed process, they got through no less than two pots of coffee, and some excellent sandwiches the office secretary had thoughtfully sent out for.

When their business was concluded, Bonnet departed with the satisfaction of knowing that his project had been put in the safe hands of the most experienced company of shipwrights in Grand Bahama.

Boarding the ferry for Nassau that evening, he considered how thrilled Morgana is sure to be, when on her return she learns of his plan for the old sailing ship.

Bonnet spent the next few days at his shipping office. He was kept busy with the drawing up of new contracts for the transporting of merchandise between the Bahama Islands and Florida, in both directions. There was so much regular trade along the eastern seaboard of the United States, and as far up the coast as Canada, that no ship of the Bonnet Line was ever left idle for so much as a single day. Other shipping companies were also thriving.

In the evenings, Bonnet took to walking around the estate, accompanied by Ratter. She had grown accustomed to her new surroundings and knew who was on duty at the gate each day. She had begun to recognize the cars belonging to regular visitors. She also enjoyed the regular meals brought to her by the cook. It was as good as being on the ship. Except, of course, there were no rats to be dispatched.

Bonnet decided one morning to take Ratter down to the waterfront. On the tether to begin with, as that would be prudent. She accompanied him from Navigation Hill all the way down to the wharf, where she quickly made friends with the port police. Docklands were, after all, familiar territory to her. She soon attracted the attention of local traders and the dock workers.

James Cuttleson had told him how she had been roaming freely on the quayside at Praia. And now, observing that no problems transpired with anyone she met here, he decided to slip the leash. It worked. Ratter just continued to follow him obediently.

He stopped at the Seagrape Bar and sat at an outside table. Ratter sat on her haunches beside him.

'What will you have, Mr. Bonnet, sir?' said the regular waiter, who was clearing glasses.

He thought for a moment and said, 'I'll have a Jack Daniels, please.'

'Anything to eat, sir?'

'Nothin' thanks. Er… Is there any chance of a bowl of water for my companion?'

'Of course. One whiskey, and one bowl of water, coming up right away!'

The waiter disappeared indoors.

Bonnet looked at Ratter and smiled. He removed his hat and placed it playfully over her tufted ears. She looked at him curiously from under the brim. It made him laugh out loud.

The waiter reappeared. Pausing at the strange spectacle, he said 'Oh, a cat in a hat, sir! That sure looks cool!' He placed the glass of whiskey on the table, put the bowl down carefully on the stone quay, and returned to his task of clearing tables.

Retrieving his hat from Ratter, Bonnet watched as she lapped up the cool water.

He sat awhile, enjoying his whiskey. Then he stretched out his legs, leaned back, and placed the hat over his eyes. He became lost in thought, knowing that Morgana's ship will most likely be nearing the British coast by now.

EIGHTEEN
REUNION

The m.v. Providence, having reached latitude 45°20'N, longitude 14°W, was now just over a day away from her destination. In this colder region the passengers no longer sat out on deck, preferring instead to remain in their individual cabins for a quiet read, or to meet with one another as they wished in the passenger bar.

That evening in the dining saloon, Captain Ferriday had the company of Caris, Chang and Cuttleson at his own table, while the chief engineer entertained Morgana, Nev and Brod at his. Stewards went back and forth bringing various dishes, while the officers and passengers chatted about anything and everything during their pleasant repast. When they had finished, they retired to the adjoining lounge for teas or coffees as they wished.

Caris, with charcoal sketches now in mind, was looking for a new subject. She hesitated before enquiring, then decided to speak up directly. 'Captain, may I do a sketch of you?'

'Yes, of course you may, Miss Meredith,' he replied. 'It isn't very often we have an artist on board.' Incidentally, Mrs. Ferriday also has a portrait of me, back home. It hangs on the wall. She did it herself some years ago.'

Caris was encouraged by the captain's response. 'When can you sit for it?'

'Well, you can do it here; right now if you wish.'

'That's marvellous!' she exclaimed. She promptly left to get her materials.

Chang and Cuttleson also left for their own cabins, as did Nev and Brod.

Morgana stayed behind. She engaged in a brief conversation with the ship's radio officer, whom she had seen at one of the other tables during the meal. She made arrangement for the following day, to go and see him in the radio room prior to the ship's arrival. Then she left the saloon and returned to her own cabin for the remainder of the evening.

The ship powered on throughout the night, with a single course correction ordered by the first mate, to keep her on the east-north-east heading.

Dawn came, ushering in the final day of the Atlantic crossing. Cuttleson was up and about early. After breakfast in the saloon he gathered his old crew together to discuss how they might, as a group, give a fitting farewell to the officers and men who had taken care of them so ably. One idea they hit upon, found favour with everyone. He then went off to speak to Captain Ferriday to inform him that, as a group "The Buccaneers" would be pleased to perform a song in the lounge after lunch. The suggestion was well received.

Lunchtime came and the group of passengers appeared, carrying their musical instruments. They deposited them in the lounge, then came and took their places in the dining saloon. La Doña Morgana made an appearance attired in her Andalusian tradition, her ropa completa. The stewards were delighted.

Caris was already there. Chang had also just seen the sketch of the Captain she had done the previous evening. She had placed it on show in the lounge. He liked it so much, he came over to her table in the saloon and asked if she would care to do one of him too, before the ship reached port. Always keen to have a new subject, Caris agreed at once.

When the meal was finished, the ship's officers followed the group into the lounge.

Chang took up his ruan, Brod his balalaika, Nev a violin that he'd borrowed from one of the seamen on the ship, and Cuttleson a tambourine given to him in Nassau by The Cool Cats.

Morgana, stepping up in front of the band, made the announcement. 'Hola! The group will sing for you an old British Navy song that is often heard around Nassau waterfront. Now we say thank you, officers of La Providencia, for bringing us safely to England.'

The Buccaneers then began a traditional song known by sailors far and wide. It would also have carried a certain resonance for Charles Bonnet, had he been present:

'Farewell and adieu to you, Spanish Lady,
Farewell and adieu to you, Lady of Spain,
For we've received orders to sail for old England,
And I hope in a short time to see you again.

We'll rant and we'll roar like true British sailors,
We'll rant and we'll roar, all across the salt seas,
Until we strike soundings in the Channel of England.
From Ushant to Scilly 'tis thirty-five leagues.

We hove our ship to, with the wind from sou'west boys,
We hove our ship to, deep soundings to take.
It's forty-five fathoms with white sandy bottom,
We bore right away boys, up the Channel to steer.

Now let every man take up his full bumper,
And let every man drink up his full glass.
For we will be jolly and drown melancholy,
And here's to the health of each true-hearted lass.'

'Let's hear it once more for The Providence!' urged Cuttleson to those who were gathered round.

The officers joined in the refrain with gusto. A couple of stewards, who never miss a trick, began miming in unison the rope hauling tasks of seamen as they all sang it once more:

> 'We'll rant and we'll roar like true British sailors,
> We'll rant and we'll roar, all across the salt seas,
> Until we strike soundings in the Channel of England.
> From Ushant to Scilly 'tis thirty-five leagues.'

At the finish, the officers whooped with delight and gave a round of applause to their enterprising passengers.

Nev left the violin with one of the stewards who was a friend of the seaman who had lent it to him, then followed the rest of the group, who all returned to the cabins with their instruments.

Once there, Chang changed into his pirate apparel and went off to sit for his portrait, while Nev and Brod rehearsed the final stage of their plan one more time. Then they too donned their colourful pirate garb, including the bandannas. They knew that the quartermaster was doing the same in his own cabin. They wanted to be attired thus, in readiness for their disembarkation at Port Guardian, where it would provide the perfect diversion. Now, it became a matter of waiting things out. They were beginning to feel all a-tingle.

A few hours later, Captain Ferriday observed in the fading light the recurring flash of the lighthouse at Lizard Point, the southernmost extremity of the British mainland. Soon, it was abeam of them. As they rounded the promontory, he gave the helmsman the order to steer north west. The lights of other vessels had by now become apparent in busy shipping lanes of the English Channel.

Morgana went to the radio room, and asked Sparks to send the message she had written for her daughter. She handed it to him, whereupon he transmitted it straightaway. A shore station then radioed back to say it had been received and had been passed on to the telegram delivery service.

Relieved to hear that this had been done, Morgana returned to her cabin. Fanny would now know that the long separation from her Mama was almost over.

With the ship's engines cut to half speed, and with the Cornish coastline to port, Bosun ordered all hands on deck to prepare for arrival. Approaching their destination after a crossing of thirteen days, the seamen were pleased to see the harbour lights coming into view at last.

Captain Ferriday gave the order to slow engines, and the second officer promptly rang the engine-room.

Shortly afterwards the ship came to rest and dropped anchor, standing off Port Guardian. The pilot station was radioed. A message came back, saying that there would be no more than a half-hour wait. Ferriday could see the stern light of another ship already on her way into port, and in the farther distance the oncoming lights of another that would come by him as she left.

Shortly afterwards Morgana, with a shawl wrapped around her shoulders, came out onto the boat deck. She could see the waterfront lights of Port Guardian clearly now, and her heart began to flutter.

Next, Cuttleson appeared, looking as piratical as the day he and his men had rescued her from captivity. He came to stand beside her at the rail and said, 'It won't be long now.'

'Sí, James. At last! My poor girl, with her Papa gone forever, and her Mama lost to her for so long. But we will be reunited at last.' She looked at him again. 'I have cried so often, thinking of her!'

'She also cried many tears, and needed to be consoled many times. I made a solemn promise to her that I would find you,' he said gently.

They stood side by side, looking across the water at the harbour lights.

'Joe was a good man,' she said sadly.

'He was indeed, and one of Charles's best captains too; but what has happened will always be there in your past, a past that cannot be altered.'

'It is true. We cannot change the past,' she said, trying to bear it bravely.

'So we look to the future,' said Cuttleson reassuringly. He paused a moment, then turned to her and said confidently: 'The future can be shaped, Morgana. A future with Charles.'

She put a hand on his shoulder, leaned forward and kissed him.

'Thank you for taking care of my daughter, James, and for saving my life. We will never forget what you have done for us.'

Chang the Chinese Pirate suddenly appeared on the boat deck, waving something he held aloft. 'Moganah! Mr. C.! Look at this!' He hurried over to them. Under the deck lighting he unrolled a large sheet of art paper. It was his portrait in charcoal, sketched skilfully by their fellow passenger. His oriental features were faithfully represented, while at the same time he was imbued with a fierce expression that suited the pirate persona. It seemed as if Chang belonged to the pages of history.

'Bravo! Es Bueno!' said Morgana, her laughter returning.

'It's marvellous!' said James, admiring Caris's style again.

'As soon as she finished, I gave to Caris a ring for payment,' said Chang proudly. 'Star Sapphire, set into gold!' He was delighted to be in possession of this exciting portrayal of himself. Rolling it up again, he returned gleefully to his cabin.

Cuttleson glanced towards the harbour again. He could now perceive in the twilight a motor launch speeding towards them. 'Here comes the pilot.'

'I need to finish packing,' said Morgana.

They quickly returned to the accommodation.

Brod was already putting his balalaika in its case. Nev's was still in its own instrument case, as he had not played it at all on the return journey. He had started thinking about getting a violin now, as he had never possessed one. The rest of the packing was nearly finished.

Cuttleson did his in no time at all. He was used to travelling light. He visited Caris's cabin and found her putting art materials away.

'Off up north then, Caris?' he asked casually.

'Yes, James. I'm going home to spend some time with my fellow artists.' She flicked back the long, wavy tresses with both hands, revealing more of the lovely face. She seemed, more than ever, to be a reincarnation of Beatrice by the River Arno.

'Take care,' he said, venturing a goodbye kiss on the porcelain cheek.

'Oh! Thank you, James,' she replied, surprised by his boldness.

He turned quickly and left the cabin.

The home she made mention of, was not her birthplace, which was in Wales. She was referring instead to the town she had lived in for the past ten years, a seaside holiday resort in the north west of England. It was an arts enclave of writers, painters, musicians, and amateur theatrical groups. She planned to go straight to the railway station after disembarkation, and from there, continue her journey up country.

Cuttleson went to see how Chang was doing and found that he had everything sorted out. The ruan was in its case and his fine silk garments were packed.

'Glad to see you are ready, Chang.'

'Aie, all done now,' Chang replied. His golden bandanna, shining under the cabin lights, proved even more striking than the quartermaster's own red bandanna and sash.

Then they heard the operation of the windlass and the grind of the anchor chain being pulled up. Evidently the pilot was aboard now. They felt the ship start to move again. As she headed into the port, Cuttleson quickly returned to his own cabin.

Morgana, still in her long skirts, white top and black shawl, reappeared on deck with her remaining luggage, which still consisted of two portmanteaux of clothes and the large canvas bag. She was, thankfully, being assisted by Nev and Brod.

The m.v. Providence was manoeuvred closer to the wharf mainly by use of her own engines, with some assistance from a tug. The pilot, glancing over the side repeatedly, gave a series of instructions from his vantage point on the bridge wing. Then he ordered 'Stop Engines'. The vessel had been given a final nudge with the precision he demanded. She was swiftly made fast and the gangway lowered.

The dockers were already standing by, ready to come aboard straightaway to get at least one hatch open and begin discharging cargo under cluster lights. They were on overtime. The ship would be spending the next twenty-four hours here, after which she would be moving on again to her next port of call, the London Docks.

The harbour pilot disembarked, and two Customs and Excise officers came aboard, as they did with all merchant vessels from whatever origin. They went to see the captain, who handed them the ship's manifest of the cargo and passengers.

The passenger group, with their documents and luggage, were taken off and escorted straight to the Customs shed. One by one, they would have to open all their luggage bags for scrutiny.

Caris was first, and Morgana came next. The searches were quickly completed, and their papers were found to be in order.

Then Cuttleson stepped forward. One of the two officers, glancing up at him and at the similarly costumed characters behind, said: 'So, what are you guys? A troupe of players?'

'Merchant seamen on leave,' said Cuttleson casually. Producing his own seaman's card and those of his companions, he handed them to the official, and added: 'We took passage as a musical troupe of entertainers on this ship. I'm the tambourine player.' He smiled as his bags were checked.

Next was Brod, who opened his.

The officer looked through the contents quickly. It had been quite a busy day for arrivals at the docks. 'What is in that?' he said, pointing to the unusually shaped case.

'Dat is balalaika. I play it,' replied Brod, looking quite casual.

'Open it and let me see.'

Brod unfastened the clasp and flipped the lid, opening it wide to display the instrument.

The officer was satisfied.

Nev went through the same procedure.

Finally, it was Chang's turn. He opened his bag for scrutiny first, and then the musical instrument case. The officer glanced at it and looked mildly curious, as he had not seen anything quite like it before.

'Now what do you call that?' he enquired.

'Chinese ruan, Sir! Like mandolin, but bigger and longer,' said Chang engagingly.

'Quite interesting,' said the officer. 'All right, you can close it again.'

The routine tasks finished, the officer looked at his colleague, who had been observing each passenger in turn as the luggage was being searched.

She nodded her agreement. 'That is quite satisfactory,' she announced. 'No duties payable. Carry on.'

The group walked off down the darkened quay, carrying all their belongings.

Morgana and the others were met by Fanny, who was accompanied by a small group of people.

'Oh, Madre de Díos! Venga a mi!' cried Morgana.

'Mama!' cried Fanny.

They fell into each other's arms, and the tears began to flow. They held each other tight.

Cuttleson had recognized the company as regulars from the tavern, but none of them apart from Fanny had realized who he was. On seeing pirates frequenting the port again, they looked momentarily disconcerted. Then he spoke up. 'Ah, you don't recognize me like this!' he said, cheerfully.

As soon as they heard his voice, one of them exclaimed: 'Well, blow me, it's Cuttleson!'

'Home from the sea again,' said another. 'So the wanderer returns.'

'It's been a long journey,' said Cuttleson.

They walked on together as a group, all chattering at once. Morgana and Fanny held hands. As they drew nearer to the tavern, they came to an old wooden sailing ship that was regularly moored at the nearby berth. The vessel had her lamps on. There was a lighted gangway that had safety rails, with sides fashioned from old sailcloth. The sides bore the advertising slogan: "Pirate Tours". At the shipboard end of the gangway, a man was standing. He was dressed in similar garb to the new arrivals. At the quayside end of it stood a young boy.

Cuttleson, to assist Morgana further, was carrying the large canvas bag that belonged to her. 'Hold hard,' he said to the others.

They all stopped as he put the bag down on the quay. He opened it and pulled out the tricorn hat. Turning to the boy, he said: 'How would you like to wear this? It used to belong to a real pirate captain.'

The boy assistant looked up at the tour manager on the gangway for his approval. The man smiled at him and nodded his agreement. Cuttleson placed the hat on the boy's head. The youngster beamed with delight.

'And a good evening to you both,' said Cuttleson, picking up the bag again.

Everyone was delighted. Walking on again, they came to the red telephone box at the corner. Caris Meredith stopped, as she wanted to make a quick call to ask for a cab to come and take her to the railway station.

The rest of the group, except for Cuttleson, continued around the corner and into the tavern. He hung back and waited until Caris had finished the call.

The two of them stood for a few minutes in the cool evening air, discussing things until the hackney cab arrived. Bathed in the light of its headlamps, they said their goodbyes. Caris kissed James on the cheek, then got in and was quickly taxied away, still waving as she disappeared.

With Caris now gone, Cuttleson entered the tavern.

The company had ordered their favourite tipples and had seated themselves in the cosy to muse over the latest developments. They had never known from Fanny herself precisely what the situation was, concerning her missing parents. Unwilling, and too unhappy to say too much to strangers, she had always resisted whenever they ventured an inquiry. Now, of course, the regulars realized that the Spanish lady who had chosen this moment to grace them with her presence, was none other than Fanny's own mother. Much as they would have liked to know more (*she might be of the nobility*), they all thought it sensible not to intrude on such an emotional reunion, and respectfully left the two of them seated over to one side, deep in conversation.

'Would you really be happy to return to Nassau, Fanny?' Morgana asked in earnest.

'Yes, I would. I will go anywhere you want me to,' replied Fanny. 'Can we return there very soon, Mama?'

'Yes, you will only need to stay a few more days at the inn where you have been living. I would like to see it for myself. Are you going to show the place to me?'

'Yes. The rooms upstairs that were rented for me by Cuttleson have been all right. I have felt safe there, knowing that he had arranged everything. He said he wanted me to stay there while he tried to discover where the island is, where Papa – .' She stopped abruptly and became tearful, so painful was the memory.

A minute passed by, and they held hands again. Then Morgana broke the silence that had descended upon them, to quickly bring her daughter back to the present. 'Could I stay at the inn with you until La Providencia returns from London?'

'Of course, Mama,' Fanny replied, wiping away the tears. 'When will the ship return?'

'Captain Ferriday has said they leave for London tomorrow, and after the rest of the cargo has been taken off there, they will start loading machinery and steel for The Bahamas. He says they will call here again in about four days' time.'

'And we can take passage then? The two of us?'

'Yes – and know this – Mr. Bonnet is in Nassau right now, waiting to see you!' She smiled at her daughter.

Fanny considered the prospect. After a few moments, she said 'You are making a new life for us, Mama?'

'A good life,' Morgana replied. 'And you will be able to go to dance school.'

'Oh, that's wonderful!' Fanny exclaimed in surprise.

'Can we go to your rooms now? There is more to tell you. Then I want you to go to bed early – and you will sleep much better from now on, I am sure. Vamos!'

'Right! We can carry some of your luggage round to the Blue Parrot ourselves. It is only a short walk. About five minutes.'

They got up and grabbed one portmanteau and the canvas bag. Morgana let James and the others know they were leaving, and they quickly departed.

Nev, Brod and Chang continued to be huddled

together as a separate group, enjoying their first drinks in England for some time. They had placed their own bags and their instruments in one corner of the room, where they could keep a watchful eye on everything.

Cuttleson continued conversing with the locals. They were attentively listening to his startling account of the storm at sea, but even with this enthralling diversion, some of them were simultaneously keeping one eye on his crew. All the tavern frequenters were still wary of piratical strangers, as their sudden presence in the port reminded them of the terrible fright Snargel had given them.

A little later, The Musician and his two associates arrived. He took stock of the group of pirates, and it did not take him long to realize that the other one chatting with the regulars was none other than Cuttleson, back again after a long absence. This put him at ease. There was no threat here.

He had a brief discussion with his fellow players regarding the set they intended to play this evening, and the choice of opener. The trio agreed on a traditional folk favourite about a historical character. Then, without so much as an introductory word to the assembled company, as he preferred his music to speak for itself, he took up the violin. The other two took up their own instruments.

The conversations in the cosy quickly died down as the audience gave the players their full attention. The strains of the violin, the flute, and the acoustic guitar began to fill the air, as the players recounted a tale of love fulfilled in the lovers' ballad, "Ned of the Hill" -

> 'Dark is the evening, silent the hour,
> Who is that minstrel by yon lonely tower?
> Whose harp is so tenderly touching with skill,
> Oh, who could it be but young Ned of the hill.
>
> He sings, Lady Love will you come with me now?
> Come and stay merrily under the bough.
> I'll pillow your head where bright fairies steal,
> If you will but marry young Ned of the hill.
>
> Young Ned of the hill has no castle, no hall,
> No bowmen or spearmen to come at his call;
> But one little archer of exquisite skill,
> Has shot a true arrow for Ned of the hill.'

The flute took up the haunting melody as they played the instrumental middle section. Then just as sweetly, all three of them sang in harmony the exquisite final stanza.

> 'It is hard to escape from this young lady's bower,
> For high is the castle and guarded the tower,
> But the mind knows the way when the heart has a will,
> And Eileen is gone with young Ned of the hill.'

As the audience broke into applause, the quartermaster came over to his fellow seafarers to say: 'Shall we take ourselves round to Fanny's place now?'

'Aye, Mr. C.' said Nev, rising quickly from his seat.

'What about dat wodka?' said Brod, staring at his glass.

'You don't need to finish it,' replied Nev. 'We can get more at the inn when we've got some rooms sorted out.'

'We go now, Brod!' said Chang, as eager as Nev to depart.

The quartet of ex-Buccaneers collected their bags and instruments, and Morgana's other portmanteau. Cuttleson gave the Musician, his fellow players, and all the taverners a general wave as they went out of the door.

Within five minutes they were at the Blue Parrot Inn. They checked in with the proprietor, who didn't even notice that one of this crew was Cuttleson, whom he had met once before, while letting rooms for young Miss Clinker on a long-stay basis. He looked the four piraticals up and down for a few moments; and then, in a manner of someone quite accustomed to reading The Riot Act to any troublemakers, said to them: 'We've 'ad your types afore in 'ere. There's to be no trouble, or it's out – an' that'll be all of you, mind – out on your ear afore you know it. Am I understood?'

Humbled, they nodded in acknowledgement. Cuttleson and the others knew when it was not in their interest to get into any arguments; and by such misadventure attract the unwelcome attention of The Law.

The check-in completed, they took their belongings up to their rooms, then came back down to the bar.

Brod asked for a bottle of vodka, and glasses for himself and Nev. Chang asked for a jug of beer from the barrel and a couple of tankards. Cuttleson asked for two bottles of the best wine the establishment could offer, and a set of five glasses. He also succeeded in getting the no-nonsense proprietor to lend him a corkscrew.

The four took their purchases upstairs to their private rooms. They also took the opportunity to change into their normal wear. The time had come to dispense with the pirate guise completely, as it had served its purpose and would not be needed again. When they were done, they reassembled in the quartermaster's room.

Cuttleson, finishing off the tankard that Chang had given him, grabbed the two wine bottles and corkscrew. 'All right, men. Fan's rooms are just at the end of the passageway. Can you bring those glasses, Brod? Ready then, Nev? Chang? Follow me.'

They went along to Fanny's with Chang bringing up the rear, carrying his instrument case. Cuttleson tapped lightly on the door.

'Hola,' said Morgana, opening it readily. 'Come in. Fan has gone to bed. She is asleep.'

'Good. The time has come to conclude this business,' said Cuttleson.

They had developed their mutually beneficial scheme with the participation of the owner of the Bonnet Line. It had been agreed that he may keep a portion of any treasure trove eventually returned by the British Museum. The ex-Buccaneers, including Tom, must also receive a share for their endeavours. Whatever is returned to Charles Bonnet in Nassau has to be divided equally. Also, the other key feature of their scheme is still in play. If, by unfortunate chance, things do not work out to their satisfaction with the British Museum, they can fall back on their failsafe provision.

Chang opened his instrument case and took out the ruan. Carefully turning it over, he placed it face down on the table. Cuttleson handed him a scrimshaw knife. Chang deftly prised open the detachable back, removed it, and revealed the contents. Five of the leather pouches.

The gems they had selected were of immense worth, perhaps even greater than the hoard of coins. Some were large uncut stones, while others had been fashioned into jewels fit for kings.

It had also been agreed by everyone that Morgana would receive one pouch, as it was by right Captain Joe Clinker's share. As they well knew, it was the spirit of her dead husband – The Wraith – that had led them to the pirate booty he had discovered.

All five individuals present also knew that a sixth pouch, already in Charles Bonnet's possession, was for young Tom. Bonnet had locked it away in a safe, in the big house on Navigation Hill. It was earmarked for the continued funding of Tom's education and his future professional training.

Chang had secured these particular pouches of gems around the inside edge of the ruan, placed away from the small sound hole of the instrument, quite out of sight of any cursory visual inspection such as that pertaining at Port Guardian. Cuttleson had rightly judged that the ruse would work here. Of the many ports around the British Isles, it was these smaller havens, situated in the far south west, that were the most useful. For centuries, this coast had been a route for contraband. It was a cat and mouse game.

The quartermaster carefully removed the pouches from their safe anchorage, and proudly distributed them, one by one, to every member of the group, including himself. Chang, by virtue of those enquiries made among dealers in Nassau, had arrived at an estimate for the gems. Its probable value was likely to be in excess of One Million Pounds Sterling on international markets.

Brod joyfully clapped his hands together in the air and danced a fine jig with Morgana. Chang cried 'Aieeeee!' and pranced about the room, delirious with excitement. Nev shook hands warmly with Cuttleson, who promptly pulled the wine corks, filled the five glasses, and called for them to be raised. He lifted his own glass and gave a toast to his shipmates:

'TO THE BUCCANEERS, AND OUR OUTSTANDINGLY SUCCESSFUL ENTERPRISE!'

EPILOGUE

Further to this account of The Buccaneer's last ocean voyage, a few more facts can be elicited for those readers who wish to know what has become of the ship and her crew, and their fellow travellers. The following information will hopefully satisfy even the most enquiring mind.

Firstly, as to what became of the old wooden ship herself. Following completion of repairs and her conversion into a floating restaurant, she was taken back to Nassau harbour, where to this day she occupies a permanent berth at the Prince George Wharf. Passengers from the cruise liners, which come and go constantly, often visit and go aboard her to enjoy the best of Bahamian cuisine. The seaborne restaurant is widely known as the "Ship-With-Two-Names". This unusual feature is the result of a special arrangement, brokered by the Bahamian government, between Charles Bonnet and the shipping registration authorities. He was given permission for the vessel to be entered on the shipping register as La Madura and as The Buccaneer. On the starboard side of the prow she bears the former name, and on the port side, the latter. Groups of diners are often seen on the fo'c'sle head, peering over one side and then the other. They crane their necks to bear witness to the fact, before going below to the old gun-deck to take their places at tables.

The gun-deck itself has a separate secured area constructed of heavy, toughened glass framed with steel, so that visitors can look through and view the one remaining portside gun. This is the cannon El Toro, which they say crippled a pirate sloop. A special licence has been granted to the ship's owner to fire blank charges from it, and the spectacle takes place at weekends, when the restaurant is guaranteed to be fully booked. El Toro proclaims its superiority by making the loudest, biggest bang that has ever been heard across Nassau's harbour by locals and visitors alike. It is a thunder which shakes the ship's timbers from stem to stern. A great cheer goes up, and diners go back to their tables calling for another round of Bahamian rum.

On national holidays, the Bonnet Shipping Company also contributes to the festive celebrations by supplying its own crew of local seamen to take the ship out of the harbour with diners aboard, sail her beyond the Paradise strip, circumnavigate it, and return them once more to the Prince George Wharf.

The restaurant owner is The Spanish Lady. She is married to Mr. Bonnet, and they have two sons. There is also a grown-up daughter who attended dance and drama school, and who is now a professional dancer in a ballet company based in Charleston, South Carolina.

Regarding our crew members who put to sea on that final ocean-going voyage of the old sailing vessel, they are now scattered to the four winds. Alexander Nevsky and Yuri Brodnov both returned to Leningrad.

Nevsky bought his own merchant ship with his newfound wealth and started his own shipping company, focused principally on the Baltic trade.

Brodnov found that despite his wealth he could not settle ashore. He returned to the sea, and in due course rose to the rank of Kapitan.

Chang Xi returned to Shanghai, in the People's Republic of China. He developed a taste for further adventure and will have a story of his own to relate. In time, you may learn of his quest for The Jade Horses.

Tom Melmerby attained his high school grades and went on to university to study marine biology. He has since published an academic paper on one of the world's longest-lived creatures, a bivalve mollusc known as the quahog. He is also dedicated to worldwide marine conservation work.

Ratter the lynx – not so young now as she once was – still lives happily on the Bonnet estate. When the Governor of the Bahama Islands eventually came to know more about her exploits, it was decided that Ratter should be awarded the Freedom of Nassau. She is often seen prowling about the quaysides wearing her neck ribbon, from which hangs a star of gold. She is quite free to roam the waterfront and is known and loved by all. Her coat is still sleek, and her tufted ears erect. She also continues to guard the perimeter of the Bonnet estate in the late hours. To this day, her eyes are as bright and as beautiful as ever.

A little more information has also come to light concerning The Wraith. Although, as already recounted to you at length, the apparition did render itself invisible to worldly sight long ago, there was a curious and unexplained incident at the wedding of Morgana de Sevilla and Charles Bonnet. She and one of her two bridesmaids, namely her own daughter Fanny Clinker, reported that a strange thing had occurred during the ceremony. Both experienced a touching, as if an invisible hand had softly rested on the shoulder for a moment. It had then stroked their hair. Neither of them reported any sense of coldness. Mother and daughter had felt a warm and loving touch.

Finally, there is James Cuttleson.

I see him clearly in my mind's eye. Imagine, if you will, my viewing him as if through a lens. He steps forward, looks in my direction and raises the salute, just as he did in Nassau.

But this time, he is not standing at the ship's rail. Instead, he stands on a road that stretches far behind him.

The salutation complete, he smiles at me – his friend and chronicler. Then he turns swiftly on his heel, and striding as purposefully as ever, he begins to take that long road.

EPILOGUE

I will surely see him again, but I know not when. It is probable that our next meeting, whenever it may be, will happen in consequence of his having completed another mission. One that he has pursued with the same vigour. Of that, I am certain. If he prevails upon me again to be the chronicler of his exploits, I will sit and listen attentively to his story.

The lone figure of James Cuttleson continues to recede into the far distance, until he reaches the vanishing point on the horizon and is lost to sight.

For exclusive discounts on Matador titles,
sign up to our occasional newsletter at
troubador.co.uk/bookshop